Greenwoman

A Literary Garden of . . .

Fiction ❋ Nonfiction ❋ Poetry ❋ Commentary
Biography ❋ Art ❋ Comics

Volume 6 - Moon Gardening

Editor-In-Chief: Sandra Knauf
Deputy Editor: Zora Knauf
Copy Editor and Advisor: Cheri Colburn
Chief Designer: Sandra Knauf
Web Designer/Tech. Support: Paul Spielman
Cover Design by Zora Knauf

Advertising contact: Sandra Knauf
719-473-9237
sandra@greenwomanmagazine.com

To purchase single copies of back issues and
digital editions online:
www.greenwomanmagazine.com

Retailers: For more information about
Greenwoman Publishing's books visit
http://www.greenwomanpublishing.com or
write sandra@greenwomanmagazine.com

Send comments, questions,
concerns, and brilliant submissions
of art and writing to: **Greenwoman
Magazine**, PO Box 6587, Colorado
Springs, CO 80934-6587

Printed in the U.S.A.

ISBN-10: 0989705692
ISBN-13: 978-0-9897056-9-1

www.greenwomanmagazine.com
www.florasforum.com
www.zeraandthegreenman.com
www.greenwomanpublishing.com

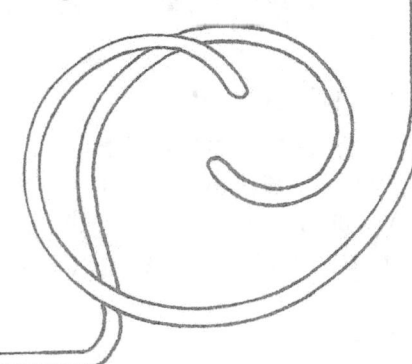

Contents

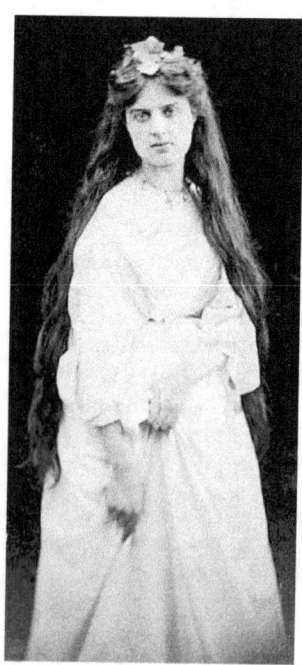

Cover art: Painting by Marie Spartali Stillman, *Madonna Pietra degli Scrovigni* (1884), adapted for our cover by Zora Knauf.

Cover Artist Marie Spartali, 1868. Photograph by Julia Margaret Cameron

Editor's Letter

Dearest readers and subscribers,

Like a band aid that needs removing, this news must be quickly told: this will be the last issue of *Greenwoman* for a while. It was an excruciating decision, but after almost four years I had to realize that when it comes to this one-woman (and when I'm lucky, two-woman) show I'm not superhuman after all. It was quite the surprise! Seriously though, I'd hoped my love for garden writing and hard work would make it happen, and it has, but not quickly enough to make it sustainable.

Building an audience is key, so that will be my focus moving forward. I am now publishing a weekly e-newsletter, based on our *Flora's Forum* blog posts. In addition to news it will link to wonderful stories, poetry, essays, artwork, book reviews, interviews and more—much like what you see here.

One thing is sure: *Greenwoman* is not going away. In fact, one of the reasons I'm letting the magazine lie fallow for a while is that we have six book projects in the works for 2014. Most are well underway (new titles and some reissues of classic works). And, as some of you know, my own novel, *Zera and the Green Man* (13 years in the making!) is out, and I must spend time on its promotion, too.

So, please stick around. Sign up for our mailing list (http://www.greenwomanmagazine.com) and see what happens next! The garden party is just starting.

Now to present this issue. Deputy Editor Zora Knauf designed the enchanting cover. I think it's fitting for the magic found within our pages. I was happy that our three fab columnists, Dan Murphy, DB Rudin, and Elisabeth Kinsey are joining us again in Issue #6; as some may know, they've all been here since the beginning. To show you that I am serious about continuing to grow *Greenwoman*, I'm introducing a new columnist, Lauri Griffin, who writes about Our Green Heritage. I hope all of these writers and other regulars, such as the incomparable Bruce Holland Rogers, will continue to be a part of *Greenwoman* via our *Flora's Forum* blog.

I'm also bursting with pleasure to share an interview with Joel Salatin, who writes most eloquently and in-depth on two of the great loves of his life, writing and publishing. We are happy to again have Sharon Rosenzweig's work grace our pages (*The Fearless Flock*, Episode 1), and last, but not least, we are honored to publish the fascinating fiction, nonfiction, and poetry of triple-threat writer/gardener/magic woman Rebekah Shardy.

Sandra

Sandra Knauf
Colorado Springs, Colorado
November, 2013

It's been a blast working with Zora (a.k.a. daughter, Deputy Editor, and "bestie").

Contributors

Born in Rochester, New York, **Laura Chilson** graduated with her BFA from SUNY Purchase School of Art+Design in 2008. She currently resides in Ithaca, NY. She specializes in pencil portraits and oil paintings and can be reached through her website, www.LauraChilson.com.

James A. Ciletti has been the Pikes Peak Poet Laureate, the president of Poetry West, and is co-owner of the independent bookstore Hooked on Books. Ciletti has published two books of poetry, won numerous awards for his work, and has debuted the first chapter of his upcoming novel in a writing magazine. He also teaches creative writing classes at the Fremont Correctional Facility.

Meredith Drake worked as a newspaper journalist and as a writer for various universities until she discovered she liked writing poetry and fiction better. She cares for her home and family in a village in western New York. Her favorite flower is currently the nasturtium.

When she's not in the garden, **Lauri Griffin** writes fiction and essays, manages a non-profit literacy program, and raises her children on homegrown vegetables. She blogs at www.laurireflections.blogspot.com, and features wall and garden art at www.etsy.com/shop/lauri-griffin.

Popular gardening blogger **Kathryn Hall** is the author of the book *Plant Whatever Brings You Joy: Blessed Wisdom from the Garden*, in which she shares 52 life lessons honed from working in many gardens over the years, each illustrated by a story from her life, designed to spark the imagination—and innate wisdom—of the reader. Her articles have appeared in *Science of Mind* magazine, *Ode Magazine*, *Bird Watcher's Digest*, *Stone Voices*, *Western North Carolina Woman*, and Garden Writer Association's *Quill and Trowel*. www.plantwhateverbringsyoujoy.com.

Pat Kennelly is a freelance writer, poet and gardener who lives and works in Colorado Springs, Colorado. Most recently her work has appeared in *The Denver Post, Haibun Today, Articus,* and *Messages from the Hidden Lake*.

Elisabeth Kinsey teaches writing online, lives in Denver, and pines away for Half Moon Bay. She has been published in *The Denver Post* and various journals. Her hands are imminently dirty. She may or may not be related to the late Dr. Alfred Kinsey.

Contributors

Leslie Macon is an oil painter living and working in Archer Lodge, North Carolina. She started as a wood carver (fashioning decoy ducks from basswood and tupelo) and switched to wildlife painting in the early '90s. After winning some awards, she began experimenting with floral and still life, and later branched out into historic portraits and visionary/fantasy art. She has had several collections published for the home décor market and some of her art has been made into licensed products. Visit her gallery at www.dailypaintworks.com/Artists/leslie-macon-3251.

Dan Murphy is a seasoned zine writer (*The Juniper, Elephant Mess*) and proponent of the slow life. His long-time passions include bike riding, skateboarding, punk rock, and gardening. His new interests include botany, ecology, wildflowers, and lichens. Dan has a B.S. in horticulture and an M.S. in biology (his thesis was on green roof technology research). He works at the Idaho Botanical Garden in Native Plant Horticulture. Learn more about Dan at www.juniperbug.blogspot.com.

Jessy Randall's poems, poetry comics, and other things have appeared in *Asimov's, MCSweeney's, Painted Bride Quarterly, Rattle,* and *West Wind.* She is a librarian at Colorado College and her website is www.personalwebs.coloradocollege.edu/~jrandall/.

Bruce Holland Rogers was born in dry, dry Tucson, Arizona, and now lives in wet, wet Eugene, Oregon. He enjoys the prospect of gardening but doesn't much like the actual work. Rogers teaches fiction writing in the MFA program of the Northwest Institute of Literary Arts. www.shortshortshort.com.

Investigative cartoonist **Sharon Rosenzweig** is passionate about backyard chickens. Fowl are outlawed in her town, so the home poultry movement has gone undercoop. Rosenzweig seeks out tales of forbidden flocks and leads readers into the netherworld of hidden hens and renegade eggs.

DB Rudin is an environmental education consultant, elementary school teacher, and the Education Coordinator at Venetucci Farm, an 190-acre historic farm in Colorado Springs, Colorado. He offers programs through Colorado Critter Encounters, which includes hands-on programs for kids on nature and conservation, and a class for those who tend the soil, The Good, the Bad and the Beautiful: Bugs 101 for Gardeners. www.cocritterencounters.com.

Rebekah Shardy, author of *98 Things A Woman Should Do in Her Lifetime*, was nominated for Excellence in Arts for Poetry by the Pikes Peak Arts Council, and was awarded first place for short fiction by Authorfest of the Rockies. In 2007, she received the "Community Builder" award from the Colorado Springs Arts, Business and Education (ABE) Consortium for creating and presenting free creative writing workshops (The Mighty Muse Writing Project for Women) to 300 survivors of domestic violence, addiction, and incarceration.

American Album Quilt, circa 1840, by Elizabeth Sanford Jennings Hopkins (1824 – 1904).
Pieced and appliqued cotton winter and floral theme quilt with embriodered, quilted details.
Collection of Denver Art Museum. Source: *Wikimedia Commons*.

Slow Life Confessions

In my youth I felt compelled to start a recycling club. I gave it a name, something clever like Recycling Rangers. I made flyers announcing meetings and bookmarks offering recycling tips. I was too timid to spread the word to anyone besides family members (who were too busy or uninterested or both), so dreams of starting my own club quickly faded.

In the 8th grade I read *Our Angry Earth* by Isaac Asimov and Frederik Pohl and that led to an English paper about saving the rainforest, which led, in 9th grade, to joining the environmental science club. Our club didn't accomplish much, but I was excited to be doing something active for the planet.

by
Dan Murphy

When I was a teen, it was the punk rock activist bands that got my attention. I became fascinated by the direct action and civil disobedience carried out by groups like Earth First! and Earth Liberation Front, and I envisioned myself as a tree sitter or demonstrating in the name of saving the planet. When I got the chance to attend my first protest in my early twenties after moving to Eugene, Oregon, I found it was pretty tame.

After high school, I studied horticulture and crop science and developed a passion for gardening. I figured that learning to grow my own food was one of the best things I could do for the environment, so that's what I did. I then went on to study green roof technology as a graduate student. I was looking for a way to combine my interest in plants with my environmentalism. Green roofs seemed like the perfect fit. Currently I work at a botanical garden caring for gardens full of native and water-wise plants while promoting the benefits of these types of gardens to the community.

Over the years my environmentalism has shifted and evolved. I have had moments of extreme thinking, like when I was feeling so anti-automobile that I was convinced that I would never own one again and that all cars should burn. The urgency that was so characteristic of my idealistic youth eventually gave way to the despondency of cynicism as I gained life experience. At times I have tried to convince myself that I should just give up the fight. But then something moves me, like watching a small, brown slug devour a tiny, purple elderberry, and I recommit myself to protecting our natural world and the precious things therein.

This passion for the environment—for living the small, simple, slow life—is in my blood. I have no other choice but to care. And so, despite the ups and downs, I press on. Certainly my approach has matured as my idealism has been tempered by realism, skepticism, and a healthy dose of cynicism, but I still care just the same. I'm still just as committed to protecting the earth as I was as a young boy attempting to start a recycling club. I just know a few more things now.

Recently I met a long-distance friend that I had known for 8 years, but only through the mail. The "me" she knew was the "me" she got to know through my zines and letters. As personal as my writing can be, that voice does not completely reflect who I am. I realized then that those who know me only through my writing may have an idea of me that is not entirely accurate. Would those people be disillusioned if they met me in person? Would they find that I am not the same guy that my writing makes me out to be?

The fear of disenchanting my pen friend welled up in me, and I found myself explaining why she might see some incongruence even before she had time to notice it (if it was even there at all). "We can only do so much," I proclaimed, "We can't do everything perfectly. We'd drive ourselves mad trying to do everything right." I was being overly defensive, but I felt like I had to defend myself, because sometimes I drive when I could bike; sometimes I forget to bring re-usable bags to the grocery store; sometimes I waste water by washing my dishes the wrong way; sometimes I buy things that aren't sustainably produced or that aren't good for me or that I don't need; sometimes I use nasty chemicals; and on and on and on. There, I said it. I'm not always the best at being environmentally responsible, and now you know.

No one is expected to be perfect though. Just because I care about the planet and write passionately about protecting it, doesn't mean that I have to be the paragon of "green." We all do what we can, realizing that we can always do better, and that's enough. Looking back on my life, I remain passionate about that inconsistent path. And so, missteps and all, I will continue to choose the slow life, just as the slow life seems to have chosen me. ❈

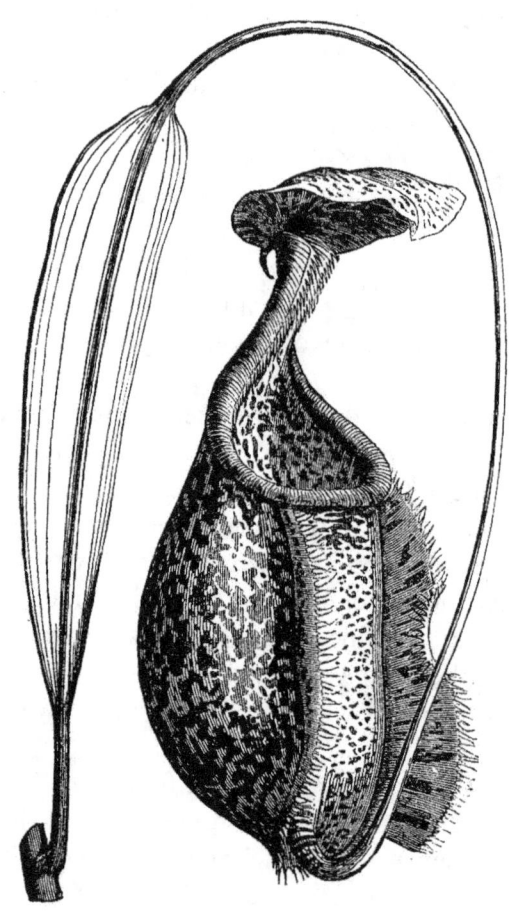

Nepenthaceae
(*Nepenthe*, pitcher plant or monkey-cup)

Johannes Carolus Bernardus (Jan) Sluijters (1881-1957)
A Vase of Tulips in Front of a Window, 1921

Canstockphoto - detail of Finland postage stamp, circa 1930.

Chopping Firewood

by James Ciletti

I love splitting wood on winter days when
air holds my face with cold hands
my mouth breathes out white sky
warm sunlight soothes my bruised bones.

I love splitting wood on winter days
when I roll these barreled stumps
to a certain distance before me,
separate my feet, and dig in my heels.

Eyeing the center ring
I raise this ax above my head,
brace it as all the ropes and
wires in my arms and back
wind and coil to strike down
this ax
again and again and again
like a fan blade wild in sunlight
until the pine crackles open
and smells clean enough to bite.

With a hand on each half
I open the log and
feel the pine
fly up into my face in flames.

Getting Your Cabbages (and Radishes, and Lettuce) in a Row
by Mae Fayne

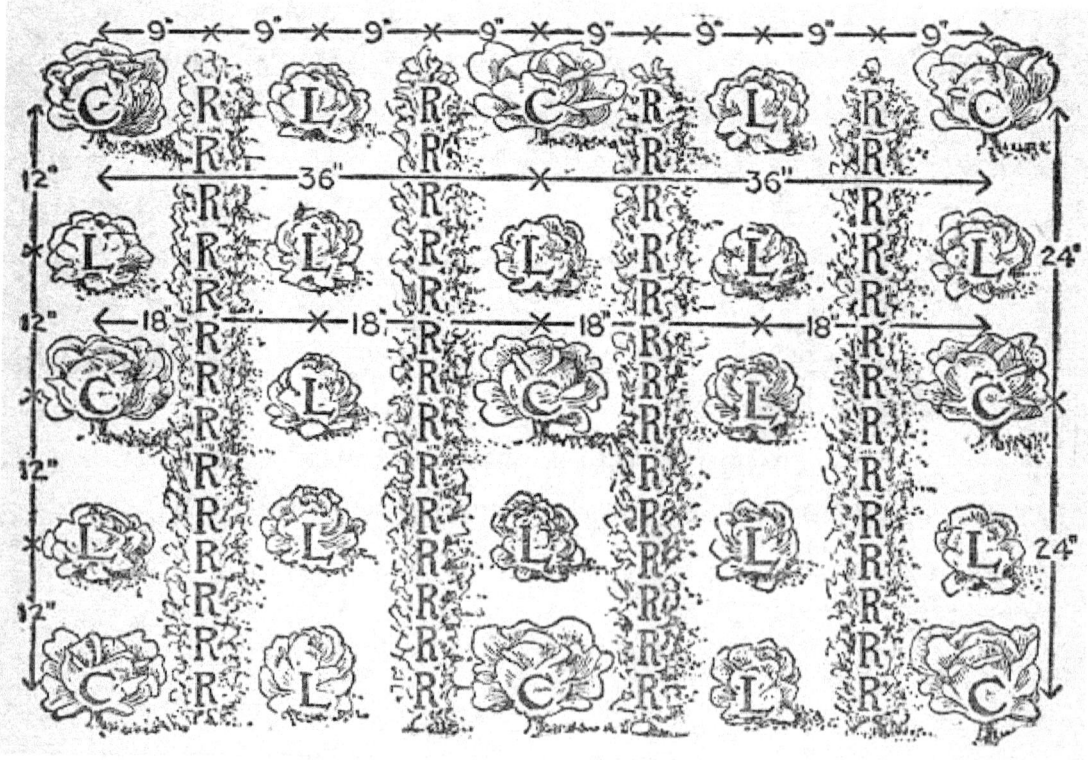

poetry comic by Jessy Randall

"Gimme Some Sugar Lil' Honey Bee" Game

by Mae Fayne & Angus Skillet

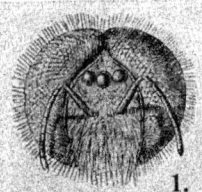
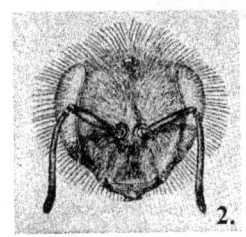
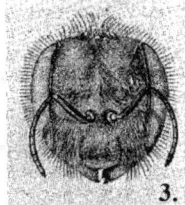

Do you know who is who in the hive?

A. The Queen = Number ____

B. The Drone = Number ____

C. The Worker = Number ____

Can you tell, by a face,
the queen from the worker
from the one
who does nothing at all
but serves as queen's lover?

Answers: A-3, B-1, C-2

Little Cabbage

by Rebekah Shardy

Illustration by Laura Chilson

"No appetite? Again?" The Nurse's Aide with impossibly long purple nails heaved the bowed old woman's wheelchair smack against the table. "You better eat those vegetables if you want to keep that girlish figure!"

That set off a gale of whoops and laughter from her friend across the room feeding a man strapped to his chair so he wouldn't fall into a bowl of gray, pureed meat.

"It ain't funny no more!" the churlish Aide focused her indignation on the woman who refused to look up, head hanging from her thick neck. "I'm getting sick of you wasting my time, Petty."

"Petty? Did you say Petty?" the other CNA asked. "You mean PATTY?"

"No, Petty. Like Pedi-gree dogfood, or pedi-cure, or pedi-phile."

"That's disgusting. What a disgusting name to give somebody."

"Sssh. They tell me she's a hospice patient. Be nice now."

The old woman, who refused to talk or even acknowledge those that talked to and about her stared at her plate. Something that had once dreamed of being a tomato lay there in a coma of yellowed, hardening flesh, its rosy juices evaporated like the old woman's last hopes.

It compelled memories from a time before days in the nursing home, before the struggle to forget the facts of her life, and the gardens that once nourished her.

* * *

She had always been too sensitive. As a girl, Emma was too shy to even look at a man, and was easily bruised by the most casual conversations. She remained single long after her siblings to end up living in her parents' old, mustard-colored stucco house at the end of Avondale Street, a content recluse at 53.

She had her delights. Standing in the rain as she weeded her garden on a hot day, feeling the rise of goosebumps from the cold pinpricks fallen on bare arms and neck. She didn't care what anyone thought as she lifted her head to taste it, the sweet-saltiness of sky and earth kissing.

Watching the paired swifts build their nests in her eaves was another joy that left her heart with inexplicable yearning. Picking scarlet raspberries, their plump soft bodies bursting in her mouth like laughter. Feeling a tentative ladybug make its intrepid way up her hairy arm to suddenly—rise! The suck and succor of new, tilled earth beneath her spreading toes, toes that instinctively kneaded the ground like a kitten does its mother for milk.

And then, like a summer storm, without warning, he came.

Her days seemed endless, mostly simple and out of doors. Indoors, she read poetry and wrote a little, but rarely entertained visitors, unless you counted the cricket she allowed entrance in the frost of fall, the caged finches she sang to at bedtime, and the one-eyed fox terrier that snored on her bed.

* * *

And then, like a summer storm, without warning, he came.

Eyes milky blue and hands too soft for a carpenter, dressed in an unfashionable yellow suit, but calm and steady enough to see her untamed, skittish soul, and love it.

He knew she was a gardener and instead of staid roses brought her bouquets of bushy tomato plants. She buried her face in their spicy leaves. When she looked up she was surprised to be greeted by a searching gaze of adoration.

"*Mon petit chou . . .*" he whispered in one blushing ear as they sat on her front porch swing at dusk.

"French?"

"*Oui.*"

"What does it mean?"

"My . . . little . . . cabbage."

She never guessed she was capable of human passion, but it followed him into her life. They never married but once she found herself pregnant; a little boy she planned to give her father's name. It was the sherry her lover brought that helped loosen her fright of conventional intimacy, the same Marsala she added to the stewed tomatoes they loved to slurp together with a dollop of sweet cream. He called them 'drunken' tomatoes—wonderful on crusty bread with lots of black pepper.

But time, which brought her pleasures unguessed, also ushered in sorrows unexpected. The child miscarried and the only man she ever loved died suddenly in an accident at the lumberyard where he sometimes searched for cast-offs. She did not live alone well anymore. Like the swifts, she wanted the safety and warmth of eaves to protect her little nest; something in her heart hissed that fall was coming.

She often thought it cruel when neighbors cut their trees in the bloom and boldness of summer, when every living thing was proud to be alive; it was in that season of abundant possibilities, 14 years after his death, that her home was taken from her.

She felt old for the first time in 73 years. Her limbs and back were too stiff and tired to garden anymore. Dark clouds of smoky wind-seeded fennel hovered ominously over the yard. Apples rotted where they fell. The berries became the birds.

"Come on, Miss Shumaker. You can't stay here now. It's not safe for you."

A nosey neighbor had complained about the little stove fire she had while napping one day. The fire department reported their concern to Adult Protection when they saw the magnitude of decline in both woman and house.

"That's not my name," she told the social worker who'd come to remove her.

"Emma, then. Come along. I found you a lovely place. They'll even cook your meals—wonderful, home-cooked food."

She wouldn't budge. "I told you: that's not my name. And I'm not going either."

"Well then, what is your name?"

Emma broke down. The sun was a starburst in a cloudless sky, and the wild sunflowers vibrated with bees on strong stalks, but she could not ignore the ruin of pale peony petals, scattered tear-like on the grass to die with her dearest memories.

"*Mon Petit chou.*"

"Mona?"

"*Petit chou.*"

"Petty? Shoe?"

All she could do was shout the truth until her cries silenced the jays in the trees and the sun covered its face in sudden clouds. "*PETIT! PETIT! PETIT!*"

"All right then," the social worker said grimly as she took Emma's arm firmly in hers. "Petty it is."

* * *

She returned to the clatter of plastic dishes being collected from the dining room tables by young women who all seemed to live with bad men, no money, and too much make-up or attitude.

Pity them, her soul said. Keep yourself secret and safe.

It was just the two of them now. The girl with purple talons also had a tattoo of a broken heart to the side of one eye like a frozen tear. It was impossible to not stare at it as the girl pulled her wheelchair close so their faces were only inches away.

"Petty. Listen. I know you can hear me. You want to go to bed?"

From the corner of her eye, there was someone in the hallway, the bright figure of a man in a lemon-colored suit.

"I said: do you want to go to sleep?"

The man impatiently moved side to side, trying to catch her eye; in his arms a vivid bunch of green leaves. Could it be?

She shocked the young woman, raising her head, looking into her eyes, mouth opened. "Yes, darling," she said, the words not intended for her. "I'm ready now." ✿

WE DIG PLANTS

LIVE Mondays at 3:30PM EST

Garden designers Carmen Devito & Alice Marcus Krieg of Groundworks Inc. delve into our human relationship with plants -- as food, medicine, fodder and as a source of beauty and inspiration. They bring the culture to horticulture and discuss such topics as botany how to, cultivation, horticultural history, garden design trends and all generally all things budding.

Check out this along with our more than 30+ live weekly shows and tons of great food news only on HeritageRadioNetwork.org

Fidelia Bridges (1834-1923)
Source: Wikimedia Commons

Still Life with Robin's Nest
Fidelia Bridges, English, 1863
Source: Wikimedia Commons

Are you and your family on the wrong side of a bet?

GENETIC ROULETTE

Movie of the year by the Solari Report & Most Transformational Film of the Year-Viewers Choice 2012.

GeneticRouletteMovie.com

presented by ResponsibleTechnology.org

MOVIE OF THE YEAR 2012
The Solari Report

VIEWER'S CHOICE 2012
Transformational Film of the Year
The AwareGuide

Cancer

Infertility

Allergies

Autism

Der neue Spielkamerad. (*The New Playmate.*) Julius Kronberg. 1873.

The Creature Feature

Arachnophilia
by DB Rudin

The battle lines are clearly drawn when it comes to spiders, with most people landing in the "intense dislike" camp. Perhaps from a contrary spirit, a fascination with biology, or even a love of *Charlotte's Web*, spider fans do exist. I admit I'm one of them. Rather than try to convince people that the 40,000 plus species of spider are worthy of love and reverence, I'm going to tell a few tales and hopefully inspire some begrudging respect and maybe a tinge of fascination for what are arguably the most successful hunters on the planet. It is the variety of ways they make a living as predators that I will primarily focus on.

Spiders belong to the class *Arachnida*, which includes other eight-legged, two-segment-bodied creatures, without antennae, like mites, scorpions and ticks. A true rogues' gallery if ever there was one.

Clearly, I'm not going to get any help making my case for spiders from their relatives. Nor am I going to get any traction trying to start a fan club for black widows, brown

> ... there are spiders that turn silk into a variety of gladiatorial-like weapons.

recluses, or tarantulas, whose dangerous venom or size and hairiness repel the masses. Perhaps I can score some points, however, for the many clever ways spiders use silk, especially in the hunt.

An individual spider can produce several different kinds of silk for different purposes: creating insect-catching webs, making egg sacs, and even building silken lairs. However silk is most commonly associated with its use, like the insect-catching web, as a hunting tool. The various other ways silk is employed may surprise you.

Beyond the sticky spiderweb catching flying insects, there are spiders that turn silk into a variety of gladiatorial-like weapons. The spitting spiders spit a liquid that is a mixture of venom and silk and congeals on contact, subduing their prey. The ogre-faced spiders, also called net-casting spiders, use huge light-collecting eyes to help find their prey in the dark. According to spider expert Dr. Linda Rayor of Cornell University, these spiders can see better at night than owls. Their hunting technique is equally fantastic as they make a stretchy silken net they hold between their front legs and actively throw it over their victims. The bolas spiders make a sticky, lariat like "rope of silk" that they swing in circles to catch their prey. This is much like the gauchos of South America swinging their bolas, or ropes with weighted balls on the end, to ensnare the legs of the animal they seek to capture. In the case of the bolas spiders, they have a blob of glue on the end of their swinging rope and they are seeking to catch moths. First, they emit the pheromone of a female moth to draw in male moths. When in striking distance they begin swinging their bolas till the glue makes contact and they can reel their victim in. As amazing as these uses of silk are, some spiders have evolved beyond them. Jumping spiders, for example, are a different cat altogether.

Jumping spiders, family *Salticidae*, include over 5,000 species who actively hunt their prey without the use of webs to ensnare them. They instead depend upon camouflage, keen eyesight, with 360 degree vision provided by their eight eyes, and the ability to pounce on their prey. They do use silk as a safety line, like mountain climbers rappelling from height when they need to bridge a gap or if they miss their target while hunting on vertical surfaces. A Google Images search of jumping spiders reveals that these diminutive hunters, (many are the size of a match head), come in an arresting array of color patterns and come as close to being "cute" as any spider can.

Then there are the *Portia*...

Portia, pronounced like the Porsche sports car, are a genus of 17 species of jumping spider. They have scientists excited about, of all things, their intelligence. All of the spiders discussed thus far, no matter how clever their hunting technique, have been working from pre-programmed genetic scripts. *Portia* spiders seem to learn from trial and error.

Dr. Simon Pollard, an expert on spiders from the University of Canterbury in New Zealand, positively gushes when describing *Portia* spiders: "They are the great leap forward in spider evolution." While employing the typical strategies of other jumping spiders, namely camouflage, keen eyesight, and the use of the pounce, *Portia* spiders take it to the next level. Again from Dr. Pollard, "From a brain no larger than a pinhead come *remarkable* hunting techniques that use patience and stealth."

They use these techniques to specialize in hunting other spiders, often much larger web-building spiders. While the web builders have poor eyesight, *Portia* spiders have extremely acute vision, superior to even other jumping spiders. They also have fast-acting venom that is especially effective against other spiders. To deploy this venom they have to first outthink their prey.

Portia spiders have been known to begin the hunt by strumming patiently on the outer strands of a web, mimicking a piece of debris. If that fails to draw in the owner of the web, they might strum more forceful- **Surely their willingness to throw themselves to the literal winds of fortune is endearing to us humans who have a penchant for exploration.** ly, imitating stuck prey or even a male web-building spider signaling its desire to mate with the female spider in the web. If in any of these cases the web builder comes to investigate, it is met with a pounce and a bite. Game over.

Sometimes a more direct approach is chosen, with the *Portia* walking across the web, somehow avoiding the sticky strands, moving only when there is a breeze to hide its approach. If this fails, the Portia might retreat and reconnoiter a new angle of attack. One fascinating bit of video footage from "Secrets and Mysteries of Spiders," (the full 51-minute video is available on YouTube), shows the *Portia* silently rappelling down, on a single silk line, from a branch above the web, then leaping when close, taking the much larger cross spider completely by surprise. Dr. Pollard summarizes his fascination with these techniques, "This type of forward thinking is almost unheard of in the invertebrate world. *Portia*'s weapon is her mind."

In the lab, Dr. Pollard has even projected an animated version of a *Portia* spider to an actual *Portia* spider. The real *Portia* is able to see and communicate with its onscreen cyber imposter. The good Dr. is literally probing into the mind of this most clever of spiders.

From the web-building black widow to the hairy tarantula, from active hunters like the jumping spiders to the mind of the *Portia* spider, spiders are more varied than first imagined. While all spiders use venom, very few pose any risk of harm to humans. In fact they provide a crucial service, controlling populations of a variety of insects, some of which could be a threat to humans if their populations were not kept in check by spiders.

Lest I leave you feeling that the interesting aspects of spider biology all have to do with hunting, spiders can also dive into the unknown with the aplomb of one of our great human explorers. On a recent autumn afternoon, I saw one of the loveliest ways spiders use silk. As I sat amongst junipers and pines, the angle of the sun, low in the afternoon sky, allowed me to see gossamer-thin threads waving in the breeze. Lilliputian spiderlings were casting their fortune with the wind with no more evolved a plan then seeking new opportunities wherever the wind happened to blow them. Scientists refer to this as ballooning. Surely their willingness to throw themselves to the literal winds of fortune is endearing to us humans who have a penchant for exploration.

So there it is, the gospel of arachnophilia, a fondness for spiders. Charlotte, in her web, and her kin could use a few more converts sympathetic to its tenets. ❀

A Few Favorites

Portia
Source: 123RF - James Anak Anthony

Deniopidae **(net-casting spider)**
Source: Louise Docker, Wikimedia Commons

Wolf spider with blowfly
Source: 123RF, Cathy Keifer

Deninopsis subrufa **(ogre-faced spider)**
Source: Jurgen Otto

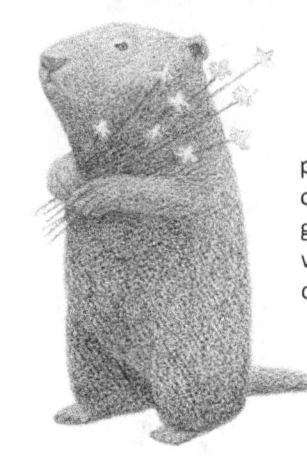

Our Green Heritage by Lauri Griffin

Heirlooms & Hothouses

Winter is a dangerous time of year for a gardener. The catalogs feature rediscovered heirloom seeds with gorgeous names: Dragon's Tongue beans, Crimson Curtain and Banana Leg tomatoes, Painted Serpent cucumbers, King of the North peppers. They sound like legends and poetry. The herbs sound like characters from old fairytales with names like feverfew, sneezewort, wormwood, and heartsease. I want them all.

It's easy to order those seed packets like candy, forgetting about the garden beds that will need digging, the soil amendments required, the weeding, the watering, the staking, and the harvesting—and forgetting that we do have limited room.

Smaller than the summer garden we dream about, is our winter greenhouse garden.

My husband got the idea from Eliot Coleman, a gardener in Maine who wrote *Four-Season Harvest* and *The Winter Harvest Handbook*. In his books he talks about how in the late 1800's, in Paris, market gardeners grew winter vegetables using horse manure from the streets to heat the greenhouses. They got the idea from methods used at Versailles in the 1670's. It makes me wonder if this history of fresh produce didn't form the French way of cooking, those luscious dishes that celebrate the foods and their flavors.

> "...what happened that it isn't standard practice for all of our houses to have a solar room to heat us in the winter and grow food for our tables?"

When my husband first starting talking about building this tall hoop tunnel for winter gardening, I could not see it working. We live in Colorado, in a semi-arid climate, at over 6,000 feet above sea level. We've been known to have -20 Fahrenheit lows, winds of 80 mph, and blizzards. And even if I did go scrape our streets, I wouldn't find horse manure.

I'd forgotten about the sun. In between those bitter cloudy days, which are few here, we have gloriously intense sunshine. The solar energy warms the soil and the air in the greenhouse. Simple. Almost magical. No electricity required. I'm amazed at how warm the sun makes the inside, it's a whole different climate—a microclimate. The air inside is thick with humidity and rich with the smell of soil and growing plants. We step inside and sigh with relief. It's a vacation from winter.

Amazingly enough, the microclimate works, though stomping through crunchy snow to go pick a salad for dinner somehow doesn't seem real. But our winter-grown lettuces, carrots, chard, and micro-greens taste amazing. The greenhouse extends our gardening season too. We are able to plant in warm soil before the rest of the garden thaws. We get tomatoes before anyone around, and we have an extra month or so in the fall for the green ones to mature.

I am amazed at this source of power, this source of growing that has been too long ignored. Sometimes it makes me angry. People as far back as the Romans had greenhouses, two thousand years ago. Where did this knowledge disappear to for so long, what happened that it isn't standard practice for all of our houses to have a solar room to heat us in the winter and grow food for our tables? Why is it considered normal and easier to haul vegetables halfway across the country to our supermarkets?

Our non-gardening friends ask us if something is wrong with our orange and yellow tomatoes, and our purple carrots. They've never seen anything like them. We've lost so many varieties, along with all that knowledge—in the name of progress, of transportation sturdiness, of convenience.

I'm encouraged, though, by how many young people are taking up gardening and by all the backyard gardens and community gardens I see sprouting up all over the country. And I'm delighted at all the varieties of vegetables that are being brought back from near-extinction. I don't know whose hands saved all these seeds, planting and harvesting them, year after year. I wish I could meet them, say thanks, and show off our garden, because I'm so grateful to grow these amazing, delicious treasures.

Although we live in the information age, we are losing wisdom as heirloom plants and long-time gardeners die off. Some treasures and knowledge are being saved, but not enough. Planting heirlooms can help keep this heritage alive. I would encourage you to buy seeds and grow a tomato bred for taste instead of transport, to plant purple carrots next spring. Share these treasures with friends and children. Keep a record of what you are learning as a gardener and pass that knowledge on. Ask those with more experience to show you how to put up the harvest for winter, or stake pole beans, or build a trellis.

I think of this quiet revolution, reclaiming a bit of our backyards along with our agricultural heritage, as I visit my winter greenhouse. Snowflakes fall outside as I pick greens that glow in the late afternoon light. As I pull a few crisp carrots for our salad out of the still-soft ground, I marvel at what we can accomplish and how much more can be done. ❉

Breton Girl Looking After Plants in the Hothouse (1884)
Anna Petersen (1845-1910)

Coping Strategies

by Bruce Holland Rogers

Leslie's life is comfortable, but the state of the world keeps her mind spinning long after she has turned out the light. She tries sleeping pills, but they make her sleep for four hours and then wake suddenly, thinking of refugees or substances in our drinking water that shouldn't be there.

A book from the library advises regular exercise, but she already jogs and swims laps. Acupuncture brings no relief. A weekly massage feels good, but still she lies awake for hours each night. At work, she tries to tally columns of numbers by hand, and the numerals swim.

A website offers strategies, such as repeating her worry until it bores her. "We are devouring the earth," she mutters to herself for half an hour in bed. She does not drop off to sleep.

A glass of wine with dinner doesn't help. Reading herself children's picture books in bed calms her only a little, and only temporarily. Leslie is going to have to resort to extreme measures. She might, for instance, wear headphones to bed and play music too loud for thinking. Thought-blasting music would keep her from sleeping at first, but maybe, eventually, she'd be able to drift off to Blitzkrieg or Metallica.

No, she's still clear-minded enough to recognize a poor strategy. She just needs to unplug all the reminders of bad news: disconnect the car radio, store away the television, cancel her subscriptions, talk to no one...

Talk is a problem. Language is the problem. Maybe she could invent a language that had no words for depletion, pollution, over-population, extinction, war, or exploitation. Unfortunately, it wouldn't suffice to have a language without the bad words. She'd have to design a grammar that couldn't express even the concept of, say, man-made climate change. Then she'd have to teach this new language to a few others, and they'd all have to foreswear any exposure to English until, through disuse, the words that kept Leslie up at night would atrophy.

She takes up a hobby instead. She crochets. Silk yarn is expensive, but she's counting on its magical properties. During her customary hours of not sleeping, she constructs a giant sleeve a little wider than her shoulders. Leslie drags herself through her days. Night after night, the sleeve grows until it is longer than Leslie is tall. At last, it's done. She wriggles into her cocoon and waits. She thinks of the wings she will have when she emerges and how she will sip from flowers, carried on the breeze.

It doesn't work. She doesn't sleep. She is not transformed. When a raging thirst drives her to wriggle out of her sanctuary, she knows that she has exhausted all strategies, the practical and the fanciful. Now, damn it, she will have to grasp at the last resort. She will have to change the world.

Photography by NASA/Apollo 17 crew; taken by either
Harison Schmitt or Ron Evans
[Public domain], via Wikimedia Commons

A Jeffersonian Agrarian Intellectual:

Greenwoman Interviews Joel Salatin on Writing

by Sandra Knauf

Illustration by Laura Chilson

As is true for most readers of garden lit, I became aware of Joel Salatin in 2006 via Michael Pollan's *The Omnivore's Dilemma*—Salatin was the cattle rancher who was doing it right. Though I knew he was an author, I have to admit that I wasn't immediately compelled to read Salatin's books. After all, I was only an urban gardener who grew a few veggies and herbs, raised a few chickens. Salatin was a real farmer.

A couple of years ago, with the local food movement in full swing (and Salatin's name on more lips than ever), I decided it was time to educate myself. I checked out *The Sheer Ecstacy of Being a Lunatic Farmer*. A couple of chapters in and a page-full of notes later, I was hooked. For Christmas 2011 I ordered four of his books, including what was then his newest, *Folks, This Ain't Normal: A Farmer's Advice for Happier Hens, Healthier People, and a Better World*. I opened it first to celebrate the New Year. Every chapter resonated. This wasn't about ranching, this was about *everything*. *Folks* covered agriculture, ranching, the food industry, our government, our culture. It was the perfect book for an urban gardener who dabbled in veggies and kept a few chickens.

As a writer, I also recognized that I was reading a book by someone who had mastered both his subject matter and the art of writing. Each page was infused with his personal experience (four decades of it), an intense (yet often humble) intelligence, insatiable curiosity, wit sometimes sharp and often playful, and an Alpha male point of view that didn't back away from criticizing government or the corporate giants. Dang. I knew right then that I had found my favorite book for 2012.

I am happy to finally share my interview with Salatin on the craft of writing in its entirety (the first half was published in 2012 in *GrowWrite! Magazine*). Salatin's since self-published another book, the one he talks about at the end of the interview, on his experiences with helping others start their own own farms. My selfish hope? That one day he'll write a book on writing and publishing.

Greenwoman: **You have a family history of farming; your father farmed and so did your grandfather. Where did the writing come from, and when did you first decide you wanted to write?**

Salatin: My mother is the theatrical communicator in our family. My paternal grandmother kept a copious diary and was known for her letter writing. My dad was extremely politically savvy and wrote so many letters to the editor of our local daily newspaper that they developed a "once a month" limit to letter writing. He cobbled together some friends who would sign his letters so he could continue to besiege the paper with his thinking, although they contained different signatures. One day the editor noticed that they were all coming from the same typewriter. Ha!

"We never had a TV in the house. We still don't."

I think I've combined my mother's dramatic talents with my dad's convictions. Mom was the high school debate coach and I grew up surrounded by her debaters in our house—and I idolized them. Our family meals included current events discussions and political issues in which Dad was interested—and writing letters to the editor.

We never had a TV in the house. We still don't. I read early, and much. Even in elementary school I would come home and sit at my desk cranking out handwritten, multi-page stories. In eighth grade, I joined the high school interscholastic debate team, competed in extemporaneous speaking, and played lead in the school plays. In college I debated intercollegiately and competed in numerous forensics tournaments.

As a junior in high school, I began working Saturday nights at the local newspaper (the one that censored Dad) as the night receptionist, answering the phone, listening to the police scanner for wrecks, fires, and crimes, and writing obituaries and police reports. I loved being "in the know." The point of all this is that from my earliest self-awareness, I had a flair for stories, embellishment, drama, and communication. It is a God-given gift and talent, honed by much practice and sharpened by excellent mentors.

Greenwoman: I read about that, your journalism work at *The News Leader*, typing obituaries and police reports while in high school. You returned to that paper for a time after graduating from college with an English degree. Why journalism? And how did that background serve you in your book writing?

"With today's publishing software, a person could create a hard news weekly that could turn the average community upside down."

Salatin: No question, the journalism work at the newspaper, both part-time during my two years in high school, and then for nearly two years after graduating college, made me the writer I am today. I also had two exceptional high school mentors. One was my senior year advanced composition teacher, whose standards for content and grammar surpassed most college English courses. I thought she was the sharpest lady in the world, and her no-nonsense approach encouraged me to excel, to be better. I had already won local essay contests and knew I had a gift for writing, but she challenged me to be better. I know she realized I had a penchant for writing, but she never let on. She just kept pushing me, and I desperately wanted to please her.

The second teacher was my high school journalism teacher and the faculty sponsor of the high school newspaper. The journalism class was also the newspaper staff. In those days, we used manual typewriters to create copy. We justified the right margin by typing slash marks at the end of each

line from the last possible character until the return bell dinged. Then we retyped the copy, counting the slash marks and inserting spaces as necessary to justify the right margin. We've come a long way, baby. Again, this teacher knew she had a live wire in me—I was already working part-time at *The News Leader*—but never coddled me. Her constant admonition: "A banana is a banana is a banana. It's never a long yellow fruit." She instilled in me a directness in speech and writing that have stood me well.

Finally, my editors at *The News Leader* made sure that my weakness toward storytelling did not cheapen the facts in news stories. I especially enjoyed muck-raking work, investigative research, and making politicians squirm. The negative was having stories spiked. It happened several times and made me ready to leave as soon as possible. Because some local politician was an officer at the Kiwanis club, or because a large advertiser's wife believed such and such, I had numerous stories spiked. Unprintable because they violated some mucky-muck.

Even today, I'm still looking for that young person to operate a hard news weekly. People do not get the news, especially from local papers where fraternization, civic clubs, and advertising relationships overwhelm the newsroom. It's the same way on a national level, but harder to correct. With today's publishing software, a person could create a hard news weekly that would turn the average community upside down. A whole network of informants would keep the phone ringing with hot tips of shenanigans to expose. In only one year I developed several informants that led me to expose things that eventually led to some powerful local bureaucrats having to resign in ignominy. That felt good.

Finally, I would say that the newspaper experiences gave me the discipline to write. When it's 11:30 and the presses run at midnight and you're feverishly finishing a late-breaking story, the editor doesn't want to hear about writer's block. Just banging it out is important. Today, when I write books, I schedule a multi-day period and immerse myself in it from dawn until bedtime, just banging through it. I'm sure other people have different techniques, but I think the discipline of newspaper work, and hard news specifically, has given me the tools to efficiently crank out material.

Greenwoman: **While America has long had a tradition of self-publishing (Benjamin Franklin and Mark Twain come immediately to mind), there seems to have been a particularly snobbish attitude toward self-publishing in America for decades and until recently. Yet, always the maverick, you've self-published seven books in the last two decades. In the unfortunate case that you don't write a book on self-publishing, would you give us your thoughts on the subject? What do you think about it and what would you say to those writers who are thinking of going down that road-less-traveled?**

Salatin: Self-publishing has been good to me. But like most things, I didn't figure it all out at once. Let's set the context. Teresa and I got married Aug. 9, 1980. I left the newspaper Sept. 24, 1982 and returned to the farm full time. Dad passed away in 1988. By that time, Teresa and I were sure the farm would make it. We weren't rich, but we sure weren't starving and we were even putting some money in the bank for savings.

In about 1989 we hosted a farm day for the Virginia Association for Biological Farming. I had edited their quarterly newsletter for a couple of years after leaving the newspaper, and then was elected president. A Pennsylvania fellow who wrote a column for the bankrupt and brand-new magazine *Stockman Grass Farmer* (*SGF*) came to that day and was so taken by our farming methods, he wrote a long article about Polyface for the magazine. The editor was so taken by the article that he called me and asked if he could come for a visit.

Allan Nation, my mentor and hero, visited in 1989 (or thereabouts—who's worried about particulars?) and immediately asked me to write columns

for him. I was overjoyed to be back writing something again after a couple of years' hiatus. He was bankrupt and couldn't pay anything, but I obliged happily. That year he hosted his first national conference and asked me to do a speech about pastured poultry. I did. It brought the house down. Suddenly we were getting calls from around the country: "How do you do this pastured poultry thing?"

> "The argument for using a publisher is always about total sales. Publishers will argue that they can sell way more than the individual because they are connected to industry standard marketing pathways. But they have to sell a LOT more to win the argument."

In 1991 I typed out a simple "Pastured Poultry Manual" and offered it for $15. Held together by brads, it was about 50 pages, regular 8 ½ x 11 typing paper, and we collated them by hand in the living room. In one year, we sold 1,000 of them, primarily through the *SGF* readership. Wow, there's money in them thar new ideas. Allan encouraged me to turn the manual into an honest-to-goodness book. Here's the awesome part: knowing my desire for value adding and do-it-yourselfing, Allan offered to either publish the book for me (the magazine operates its own in-house publishing brand called Green Park Press) or shepherd me into doing it myself. Once I found out that the author got less than 10 percent of the cover price, I couldn't imagine having him publish it.

After all, I'd just taken in $15,000 on a simple loose-leaf how-to manual; why would I trade that for $1,500? Allan and his wife Carolyn were as good as their word, sending me sample bid sheets, particulars on ISB numbers, Library of Congress, and potential short-run paperback book printers. I typed the manuscript on the typewriter and sent it to a friend who could make a camera-ready copy. In 1993, we self-published *Pastured Poultry Profits: Net $25,000 in 6 months on 20 Acres*. Now nearly 20 years later, it is still selling better than ever, with total sales about $60,000.

> "I always tell people considering self-publishing to get their name out there first. Write articles, do speeches, something to get name recognition. Then the book sales will follow."

The argument for using a publisher is always about total sales. Publishers will argue that they can sell way more than the individual because they are connected to industry standard marketing pathways. But they have to sell a LOT more to win the argument. I knew this how-to book would not be a best seller, so I figured I'd rather sell 30,000 at a $10 margin than 60,000 at a $2 margin. That assuming, of course, that the publisher actually doubles your sales.

Notice that before self-publishing I already had a following. I was writing columns in *SGF*, speaking at conferences, and was considered the go-to expert, worldwide, on pastured poultry. That was a huge leg up. I always tell people considering self-publishing to get their name out there first. Write articles, do speeches, something to get name recognition. Then the book sales will follow. Remember, half of all books ever published in history have never sold more than 1,000 copies. That's tough odds unless you have an incredible talent (Dr. Seuss) or an incredible idea (pastured poultry).

Self-publishing has become much easier with desktop publishing software, PDF, and everything computer-based. Interestingly, many of the old bricks-and-mortar marketing pathways are also breaking down. After *Salad Bar Beef* came out in 1995, Ben Watson at Chelsea Green Publishing saw the two books at a conference in New England, took them home, and realized these were exactly the kind of books Chelsea liked to handle. He called me and asked if they could distribute them. I became a distributed publisher for Chelsea and it was one of the best decisions I could have ever made.

Chelsea handles bookstores, libraries, schools, Amazon.com, etc. *SGF* doesn't handle any of my books anymore

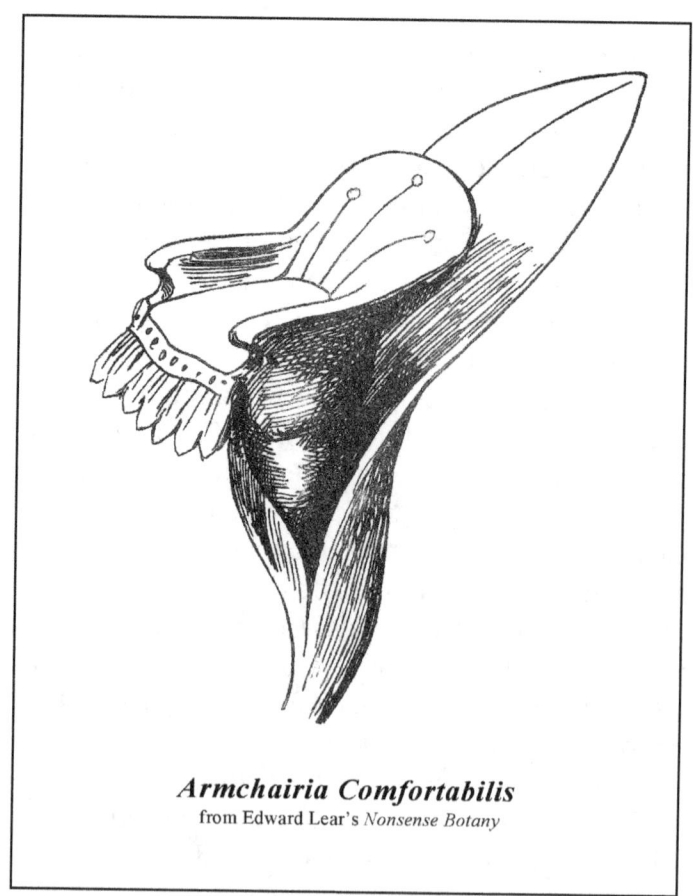

Armchairia Comfortabilis
from Edward Lear's *Nonsense Botany*

because Amazon undersells them. Allan has made a strategic decision not to allow any of his Green Park Press books on Amazon—if you want one of his several titles, you have to get it from *SGF* or *ACRES USA* magazine, another of my special media friends. Allan and I have gone around and around about my decision to let Amazon carry my books versus his decision to not participate. Neither side is right or wrong. I'm frustrated that Amazon has so changed the face of book marketing. But I've gone with the times and am very pleased. My Chelsea checks today are 10 times bigger each month than they were from *SGF* bookshelf section. Have I sold my soul? Time will tell. I hope not.

I think I'm Chelsea's number one distributed publisher now. My only beef with them is that they don't really market books they don't publish. They offer them in their catalogue and ship them, but nobody actively markets them. The advantage to me, of course, is that I don't have to worry about all that shipping and packing. If I were more computer savvy and wanted to hire someone to do it, I probably could, but I don't want to. That's not my talent. So I help employ people at Chelsea and they write me a nice big check every month. Seems like a good tradeoff to me. I don't think my reach or success would be half as far without them.

The last self-published book we did, *The Sheer Ecstasy of Being a Lunatic Farmer* (late 2010) has already sold nearly 20,000 without a single review or any marketing effort. I am blessed indeed.

Greenwoman: How is your newest book, *Folks, This Ain't Normal*, published by Center Street, different from your self-published books?

Salatin: It was certainly wonderful to work with an editor. I've never had a really good, hard-hitting editor. It's definitely the best book yet. Lots of my faithful readers say it flows better, is more cogent, etc. That's good editing. If I self-publish the next one, which I probably will, I'm definitely planning to find an editor who will yell at me. I'm thinking one of my old high school teachers would be good—they've both retired now, but are still in the area. Friends just won't be honest because they are too afraid of offending. You need someone that's impartial. I know the good editor made it a much stronger book.

Fortunately, my biggest fear—that they would force me into political correctness—did not occur. Again, my fans say they can't tell the content and overall style is any different than any of my other books. That was a relief.

Greenwoman: Who are your favorite authors—and why?

Salatin: My favorite authors—that's hard. So many great ones. Probably the writer I most admired was Charles Walters, editor and founder of *Acres USA*

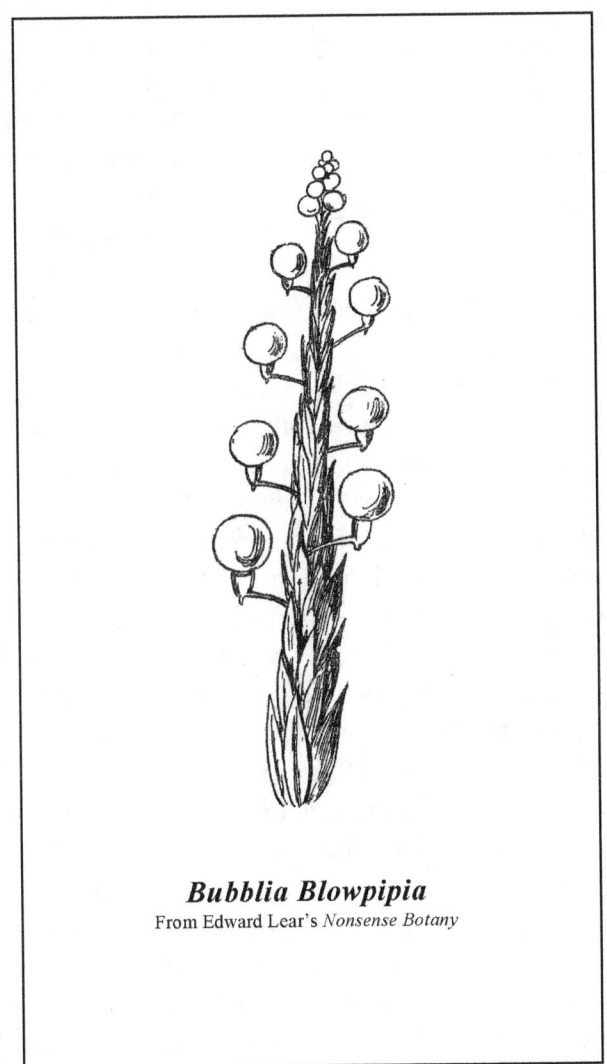

Bubblia Blowpipia
From Edward Lear's *Nonsense Botany*

magazine who passed away two years ago. His command of the English language, his depth of literary understanding was so far beyond anyone I know that I was in awe every time I read his stuff. Here's one of my favorites: "monuments to the stupidity of man" —his description of pesticides, etc. "Toxic rescue chemistry"—chemical-based farming. He was a wordsmith beyond anything we'll probably see again. His grasp of literature, both English, classic, mythical, European—was incredible. I miss him terribly.

Second is probably Wendell Berry. Whenever I read him, I'm constantly saying to myself: "Now why couldn't I think of that?" Arguably the voice and founder of the modern sustainable agriculture movement, or the new agrarianism, he writes simply and clearly, an elegance that never leaves you wondering what he means or what he said. He writes roughly 3-4 hours every day with a number two pencil in his tree house studio on the bank of a wide river. He writes on the right side of a spiral notebook. The next day, he reads what he wrote and makes corrections on the blank left page. Then his wife or assistant types what he wrote. Some 57 books and counting —not bad for a number 2 pencil in a spiral notebook.

Third is Allan Nation, editor of *Stockman Grass Farmer* magazine, not really for his writing style, but for his eclectic approach. Allan reads a book a day, and he reads widely. From history to business to railroads to farming, the depth and breadth he brings to my world refreshes and challenges me. I always tell people I'm trying to be a "Jeffersonian intellectual agrarian." Allan's writing helps me be intellectual. When I use his distilled ideas, people think I'm extremely smart. I'm not really smart; I just have a talent for knowing who to plagiarize.

Fourth is Sir Albert Howard, inventor and researcher, who developed scientific aerobic composting and explained it to the world in An Agricultural Testament in 1943. Of all the classic biological farming texts, Howard's works are both timeless and passionate. He doesn't write like a scientist. He writes like a lover of life. Probably more than any other writer, he created a fire in my belly to love the land, love the life in and around us, and to question every credentialed scientific finding from government sources.

Fifth is George Henderson, whose *Farming Ladder* book grew out of his own entrepreneurial farming experiences in Great Britain during the mid-20th century. A wonderful writer, he was eccentric enough to be a genius, yet practical enough to be duplicated. He is a farmer's farmer, writing from the heart but with fingers calloused and muscles hardened through use.

Sixth is Charles Dickens. I read so much—as the previous list attests—for my life's work, my own understanding of my vocation and craft, that sometimes I want to take a detour. I don't read much fiction, but have found great enjoyment in the classics. I never read them in school because my reading pleasure always involved debate research. So at this point in my life, I've discovered the great classics and am captivated by the power of their stories. In my opinion, no one captivates me like Charles Dickens. And to think he wrote with a quill pen. I read *David Copperfield* on my last trip back from Australia—14 hours on one flight. I didn't go to the bathroom, sleep, or get tired. The story was absolutely consuming. I laughed and cried as I lived this wonderful tale leaping out to my imagination, across the decades, across the cultures. His ability to criticize his culture is unparalleled. I wish I could make up a yarn like Dickens.

"Does reading your words aloud to yourself evoke emotion? Do you laugh? Cry? Get angry? Want to do something right now? If your own writing does not move you, it won't move anyone else."

Greenwoman: What do you think has played the biggest part in your book selling success (aside from writing great books)?

Salatin: Passion. Writing from the heart. Wanting, above all else, for people to act right, do right, think right. I believe strongly that there are right ways and wrong ways. I certainly don't have an opinion about everything, and in my books I mention some of them that I frankly don't know what position to take. But I have strong beliefs about a few things, and those I passionately articulate.

I think one of the most important elements of good writing is openness. The reason nobody likes to read bureaucratic stuff is because it can never be transparent. People who write that stuff have to be wordy and unclear because they are always thinking about a hundred agendas that must be satisfied. I think my strength is just expressing my Joelness. I'm a passionate defender of the pigness of the pig. A corollary is the Joelness of Joel. You might not like me, but at least you'll know who I am, where I stand, and that I'm trying to think and do the right things.

Perhaps the second reason for my success is that I always write for someone, or to someone. I'm always thinking: "How can I sound bite this more clearly, more cleverly?" I'm an idea salesman. Marketers are always working at saying it simpler. Making the message fun. Creating a good time. Theater. I don't call my speeches lectures; I call them performances. I love it when someone tells me at a book signing that they feel like they know me, like they've been sitting down just talking with me through the written word. I assume that posture when I write—like I'm sitting with the reader and we're having a conversation on the sofa in front of a fire. I find that helps me be conversational and real.

When I've tutored young people on writing, I always tell them to read their paper back to themselves in front of a mirror. If you find yourself boring or confusing, so will your reader. Does reading your words aloud to yourself evoke emotion? Do you laugh? Cry? Get angry? Want to do something right now? If your own writing does not move you, it won't move anyone else.

Do not write anything until you're moved about something. We live in such a wimpy culture, where strength of idea is routinely wrestled down to some weak common denominator. I think people like strong ideas, strong pictures. Great writers have deep ideas that move them and consequently have the power to move others. If what you want to write about really moves you—if you'd rather talk about it than eat—then you're ready to write. When you write, don't think that it's anything different than a conversation. I've never understood how people who could prattle on for an hour suddenly clam up with a pencil in their hand? What's any different about writing than talking? Perhaps it's the gravity of indelible history. Of commitment. But really, it's a written record of a conversation. Often a one-way conversation to be sure, but a conversation nonetheless.

> "I think people like strong ideas, strong pictures. Great writers have deep ideas that move them and consequently have the power to move others. If what you want to write about really moves you—if you'd rather talk about it than eat—then you're ready to write."

Greenwoman: What advice would you give to authors in regard to promotion/sales?

Salatin: You have to be both expert and showman. Look at the talk shows, both radio and TV. You can't be mediocre about your craft. I read constantly, and I mean constantly, to stay up-do-date with farming, food, economics, etc. My reporter background stands me well when I meet people because I'm always asking questions. This is what struck me about Michael Pollan when he came to the farm prior to writing *Omnivore's Dilemma*. I've routinely described him as a curious 8-year-old in a grown-up body. But that's how he finds the tidbits that make for a great story.

I wish I had better advice for sales. Really, I haven't marketed my books at all. They've just sold because they scratched people where they itched. I'm sure I could have sold more if I did more active promotion, but I've always been a bit scared of anyone thinking I'm in it for the money. As a little child, I stole some money, and I've never gotten over it—the heartbreak and agony of it, from punishment to restitution. I wish I could live without money. I've never wanted to be rich. I still wear thrift store clothes on the farm. I'm naive enough to think that people still salute powerful ideas, truth, and righteousness.

Greenwoman: **I've read that you write during the winter, when the farm is not quite as active. What is your writing regimen?**

Salatin: I think I answered this earlier with the daylight to bedtime regimen. It's intense. All my books have been written in a few days. The longest, *You Can Farm*, took nearly 6 weeks. *Folks, This Ain't Normal* took just under 3 weeks. I create a chapter outline, then set a goal for the day: these two chapters, or whatever. Then I just march through. I have my stack of stuff that I've been collecting for a year or so, and plug it in as I come to it. It's very much stream-of-consciousness type stuff.

But remember, by the time I actually write, I've been stewing, meditating, talking about this topic for years. The outline gives me a skeleton and a direction. A book is never actually finished. You can edit forever. I find that if I just crank through it, let it sit for two weeks or so, then go back through to add in things I've missed, or take out repetitive things, it doesn't do any good to just go over and over and over. Perhaps growing up with a manual typewriter helped me to think through things before I write. At any rate, I always figure that if I forgot something, I can put it in the next book.

The wonderful thing about books is that it's the only medium I know of where I can truly develop a thought. A magazine article does not afford the time. Video definitely does not afford the time. We live in a sound bite culture. But a book allows me unfettered time to look at every angle. I can't believe the number of people who have told me they've changed their thinking because of my books—people I know who would never give an idea the time of day in a magazine or on a TV show. But in a book I can lead up to it, set context, admit the other sides. If it takes 20 pages to develop the idea, so be it. If these pages are full of story, they will compel the reader to stay with it to the bitter end. Story is still the most powerful type of persuasion. Story that requires you to use your imagination because it's not all laid out in 3-D and color forces more thinking, more engagement, and ultimately, a deeper relationship.

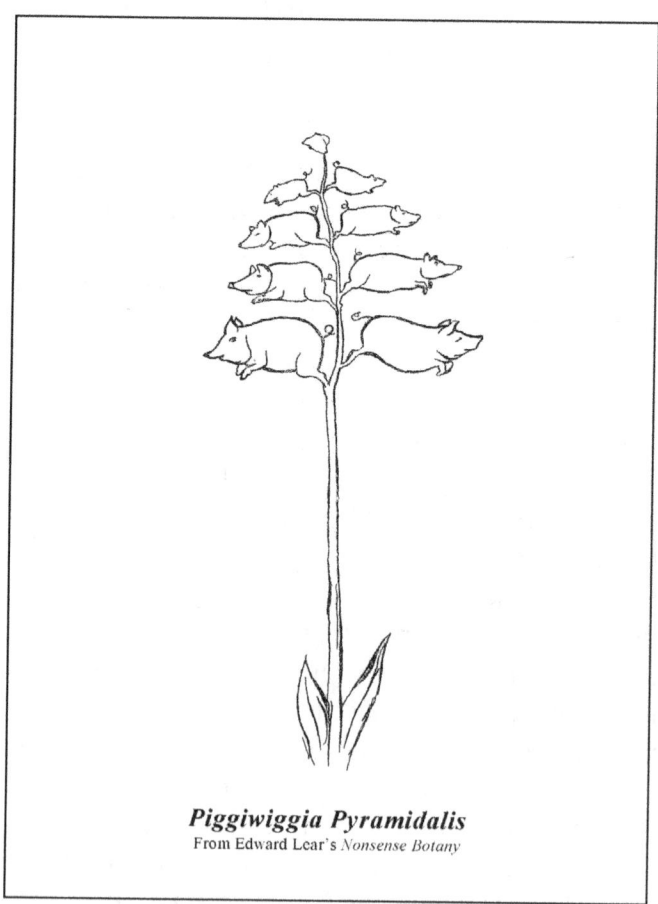

Piggiwiggia Pyramidalis
From Edward Lear's *Nonsense Botany*

Greenwoman: **What is your favorite book out of the eight you have now published, and why?**

Salatin: *Folks, This Ain't Normal* because it's the last one. The last one always benefits from the highest evolution of thought, the greatest number of stories, the deepest wisdom of age. That said, each is very different. *You Can Farm* is by far and away the biggest seller. *But Everything I Want to Do is Illegal* is the most important, in my view. It's the one everyone needs to read more than any other.

The Sheer Ecstasy of Being a Lunatic Farmer was the most fun to write. It's probably the funniest. And lots of non-farmers read it for pure enjoyment. If you ever wanted to know how to look at a rural landscape with discernment, this is the book.

Finally *Family Friendly Farming* is my soul book. It has sold the least copies—only about 12,000. I thought it would be gobbled up by the homeschooling crowd, but it has languished. I don't know if it's because the topic is too personal. Perhaps most people think their family can't be improved, or if they buy it, they are admitting it can't be improved. But it's the closest to my soul.

Greenwoman: **Do you know what you'll be writing about next?**

Salatin: I have about 8 titles dancing in my head, but I think the one that's most pressing is about internships, apprenticeships, and mentoring. As this local food tsunami gains strength, thousands of young people want to learn how to farm. Institutions can't or won't teach these skills.

Because we homeschooled our own children—when parents were being taken to jail for truancy violations—I am steeped in non-institutional education-think. I am always fascinated by how people learn things. And being pretty libertarian, my independent rebellious streak has always had trouble submitting to institutional protocols like "because I say so."

Everywhere I travel, farmers are desperate to institute intern programs. Young people want to learn. I believe I've been uniquely prepared, both by experience and interest, to address this topic in a vibrant, pro-active, yet highly practical way. I wrote a little pocket-sized apprentice manual for our Polyface folks a couple of years ago, and whenever I bring it out and share it at a long seminar—the only kind that allow the time to delve into this subject —the audience howls with laughter. Afterward, people mob me to see if they can get a copy. So I know it's a hot topic, which sounds like a market. Time to sell some more ideas. ❋

Joel Salatin's Books

Salad Bar Beef (1996)
Pastured Poultry Profit$ (1996)
You Can Farm: The Entrepreneur's Guide to Start & Succeed in a Farming Enterprise (1998)
Family Friendly Farming: A Multigenerational Home-Based Business Testament (2001)
Holy Cows and Hog Heaven: The Food Buyer's Guide To Farm Friendly Food (2005)
Everything I Want To Do Is Illegal: War Stories From the Local Food Front (2007)
The Sheer Ecstasy of Being a Lunatic Farmer (2010)
Folks, This Ain't Normal: A Farmer's Advice for Happier Hens, Healthier People, and a Better World (Center Street, 2011)
Fields of Farmers: Interning, Mentoring, Partnering, Germinating (Polyface, 2013)

Natural Magic by Eleanor Fortescue Brickdale, 1905

Love & Roses
by Sandra Knauf

"You've got to be kidding," I said as I cleared the breakfast dishes, "you can't work again this weekend."

"I have to. I have to finish this job."

"But you worked last Saturday, and the Saturday before. I can't remember the last time you spent a whole weekend at home! Come on, don't leave me with the kids again."

He poured another cup of coffee. "Do you think I like working all the time? I'd rather be home with you."

It doesn't feel that way. Hurt blooms in me, escaping in the form of anger. "Maybe you shouldn't work for yourself. I know plenty of people who don't and they have weekends off, vacations, even, if you can imagine that."

"I'll never work for someone else again. I like working for myself."

"And I'm left with the kids, constantly." I glared at him. "I feel like a single mom."

"Maybe you should get an outside job."

"Yeah, and you could hire a bookkeeper, and we could put the girls in day care—and you could do half the work around here too, cook the meals, take care of the yard, the pets, the bills. Sounds pretty sweet to me."

The situation deteriorated. We smacked each other around verbally on the issues of parenting, money-spending habits, neglected chores. My mind was a red fog of betrayal—all I could think was: He's abandoning me again. A beautiful Saturday in May, and I'm going to be alone with the kids.

The fight ended with a hissed, "I fucking hate you!" from me as I stormed out the back door, slamming it.

It was good the girls were still asleep or they would have witnessed another fine display of parental maturity; that thought brought shame. Contrary to my hateful words, I did not hate my husband, and I knew he wasn't trying to hurt me. We were just stressed-out parents with a lot of responsibilities, trying to keep a roof over our heads, fighting to swim in that upstream river of life, and to not give in to the more than occasional emotions of suffocation and isolation.

* * *

I walk into the garden and the dewy yet crisp Colorado air envelopes me like a balm. I don't notice. What I do notice is that there are a million chores outside too. My irritation surges again before the escape, the changed atmosphere, begins to sink in and slowly soothe.

I look around and decide to work on the rustic arch I'm building, a project that came about after my husband took down four small too-close-to-the-house weed trees. While I wasn't happy to see the trees go, I knew just what to do with them, how they'd fit into the scheme of our cottage garden. The day before I had dug the post holes, two foot deep into our clay soil, and set the branchless trunks as posts. Today I'd work on connecting it all with the branches I'd removed.

After almost an hour of sawing, nailing and wiring, enjoying the exertion and creation, my tension and hurts have mostly, but not totally, melted. I step back and admire my incomplete handiwork. How I love rustic garden structures. The imperfection, asymmetry, and the roughness all appeal to me because those qualities mirror my own untamed gardening style. The arch also works well with our DIY budget and, I think, with the style of the 1920s bungalow. I study the sturdy arch, my first. It's pleasant to the eye, and I am surprised. I've never been mechanically inclined, yet . . . I did it! I'm happier now, partially cleansed of bad feelings. I consider going in and trying to make amends. I'll finish the arch later, after I've had time to reflect on its developing form.

As I gather up tools and head toward the house, I notice the tall rose canes covering the side of my husband's workshop, our old one-car garage. Eyeing the brambles, I think, with no small shame, how the dead wood outnumbers the living. Three years of intense drought and neglect on my part has taken its toll. The shrubs, a hardy antique variety planted decades earlier by another, nearly scream, "Over here, help us!" I have handsaw and pruners in hand, but I am gloveless and sleeveless. I look at the house and push away the thought of going inside. I'm not ready. Not yet.

I begin cautiously, with some dead canes, the ones I can safely saw without actually entering the briars. It goes well. This isn't difficult, I think, you just have to pay close attention—I probably don't even need gloves. The thorned old wood begins to pile up in a heap. I take a deep breath and smile to myself. I move in closer.

I soon earn a couple of scratches, but I'm engaged in my work and reluctant to stop. After a few more, I begin to wonder if I have a not-so-latent masochistic aspect to my personality. The scratches on my arm sting slightly,

> "My mind wanders to those souls who actually enjoy pain. I imagine the Marquis de Sade would relish the thought of bare-skinned rose pruning. He'd dispense with *all* the clothing."

softly singing in agreement ("You're a little weird . . . oh, yes, you are.") My mind wanders to those souls who actually enjoy pain. I imagine the Marquis de Sade would relish the thought of bare-skinned rose pruning. He'd dispense with *all* the clothing. But I'm not the Marquis. I'm just impulsive and have a higher pain threshold than most, and besides, I'm making such progress. The truth is I'm still not ready to face my husband. If I go inside now, to a house full of family and demands, it will be hard to return to these canes—and I am so enjoying this solitude and productivity.

Gingerly, I squeeze in deeper, past a gentle honeysuckle who will do me no harm. I am in the thicket. I find myself wedged between the garage and the roses, with only a couple of feet in which to maneuver. It's darker here, like a medieval forest. The morning, still young, is cool in these shadows, the air fresh. The canes are beginning to leaf out, the birds are singing. It's lovely, and I begin to forget about the scratches. Then, I discover the dead wood here is especially hard and thick and the thorns menacing. After another ten minutes of exertion and yet another bloody scratch, I begin to imagine that they are consciously vicious. The thorns resemble sharp, curved talons. Dragon's claws.

That image, wed with the romantic dappled light, conjures fairy stories. I think about the briars that held Sleeping Beauty's kingdom captive for one hundred years. They too were treacherous, all enclosing. I start at a sharp pain and draw back—a large thorn is impaled on the tip of my index finger. Could this be Nature's retribution for the lover's quarrel? Wincing, I pull the thorn out and the garnet blood makes a jewel drop on my skin. I stick the injured finger into my mouth and immediately think of Aurora, Sleeping Beauty. Surely this is how she must have felt when pricked by the spinning wheel. The almost-premonition of a stab, then, too late, it is done. The deep sleep begins. Only after a century, and numerous bloody, failed attempts by velvet-cloaked suitors, is the true prince able to enter and awaken her. The protective brambles part for him, he is blessed.

I move thoughtfully now, wielding my slender saw like a sword, my mind now focused on consideration and good thoughts for the roses—these exquisite sentinels. This is how the green prince of kisses would think, I am sure of it.

I do not get scratched now.

Soon these canes will be covered with soft baby buds, pale pinkish-cream, cradled by endearing dark green sepals. These symbols of youth (gather ye rosebuds) will grow, swell, and open into almost luminescent-white blossoms with a spicy, lemony scent. Full blown, hardy, irresistible roses, so much like blossoming young women. Soon they'll be wide awake and ready for pollination. I think of how, in years with rain, these canes have exploded. I have laughed out loud at the sight of greedy squirrels stuffing whole blooms into their mouths. Snow-white flowers, rose-red blood. As I prune and saw, my mind begins to make more associations between love and roses. Do roses really mean love?

Well, new love is heady, and like attar of roses, bears no comparison. Like perfume, like a dream, it can engulf us, make us unaware of the outside world, to everything but itself. New love reminds me of a selfish, pampered, hot house tea rose, a Miss America bouquet, stripped of its thorns, nestled in tissue paper, put in a box and wrapped with a big bow. I remember how my husband and I, so young, once bloomed as hot and perfect as those tea roses. In our springtime, those years together before becoming parents, we had few cares and fewer thoughts of the future. We were content to revel in one another. Now I know that early type of love is fleeting, too precious for the rigors of time, too fragile for hardship to last. I've seen those pampered rose bouquets. Sometimes the blossoms die before they even open.

I recall my horrible words. The thorns. The flip side of love. The opposite of those velvety, color-soaked, petals strewn on beds of love. The slashings of reality, the smothering trials of everyday life. I think of how all love has thorns, and how some can scar for life. I have seen love as destroyer in my own family and with friends. Roses of Delusion. Delusions of who we are, who our lovers are. I have seen the thorns that destroyed Aurora's other suitors for a hundred years destroy others; I have felt thorns that, a few times, have come close to destroying my own love.

"You've made quite a pile there."

Frowning at the difficulties of love, I didn't notice that my husband had walked up and was watching me.

I peer through the greenery, smiling awkwardly at the handsome king, and wipe the sweat from my brow. "Yeah, I kind of went crazy. I'm pretty scratched up, but I've just about finished. It looks a lot better, don't you think?"

"It looks great. I'll help you get those canes in the Dumpster."

"Really?" I wiggle out. "Thanks."

We've apologized the way we always do, without words. As he walks away, hauling a bundle of dead canes, I contemplate the roses I've pruned. The antique roses, hardy, with ancient, wild parentage, are built to last, so unlike the pampered hybrid teas. In fact, there are antique roses in Europe, still living, that bloomed during the time of the Brothers Grimm, and in France, Josephine's rose garden survives. While there are never guarantees that love will survive, I feel that through the stings and scrapes of life, the love I share with this man has proved to be a variety that through drought and hardship, will insist on living and blooming, year after year, rooted deeply, tenaciously, into the soil. ❀

BACKYARD CHICKENS are back in style. Martha Stewart keeps them and Williams Sonoma sells swanky coops. Yet some city councils, succumbing to fowl fears of falling property values and predators, have made the practice illegal, hatching an underworld of renegades.

UNDERCOVER REPORTER, HENRIETTA CHOOKS, investigates the PIONEERS of POULTRY, hiding the HENS of HIGHLAND PARK. Who are they? What motivates them?

The stories are TRUE, but the names have been changed to protect the feathered.

EPISODE ONE: The FEARLESS FLOCK

They ain't chicken!

Hi, I'm the undercoop investigator you spoke with.

Yes, come have a look!

I brought them some lettuce from the dumpster behind FAMOUS FOODS.

Thanks, they FORAGE all the time, but they don't find much GREEN in February.

SKWAAK!

Garden Party

by Meredith Drake

The weeds in my garden
awake in their seed pods,
squat in their steamy caves,
dip their feet in the dung.

The weeds in my garden
linger at the soil line,
slim silent serving girls,
slender arms wrapped
around their waists,
collars buttoned to their chins.

Summoned by sun,
the weeds in my garden
leap from the soil,
wave their shirts at my house,
surge up the flower stalks,
merry brigands in the rigging.

The weeds in my garden
stoop to weep over the romas
whose bellies won't swell
into fat mandolins.

The weeds in my garden
stagger in their crowns,
toss their coins to the soil.

The weeds in my garden
brawl in the walkways,
fall tipsy and sprawling,
lay dormant, then dead.

New weeds in my garden,
are swaddled in seed pods,
new nurslings in buntings,
in slumber 'til spring.

123RF Kristina Afanasyeva

Sadie & Ruby ♥ Greenwoman Magazine

(& Zera and the Green Man, & Greenwoman Publishing's books, & Flora's Forum . . .)

Sadie: Now what are we going to do? *Greenwoman*'s not going to be around for a while . . . life's not going to be the same!

Ruby: Never fear, Sadie. *Greenwoman* is not only a magazine. It's a book publishing company and more! Have you read ***Zera and the Green Man***? It's another mind-blowing experience. They have more cool books coming out this winter and spring. Then there are these great weekly blog posts on Flora's Forum . . . it's just like ***Greenwoman Magazine***, only in small, delicious doses!

Sadie: Well, heck, I guess I'll try not to be too sad then . . .

Ruby: No reason to be. *Greenwoman* is just getting started!

Sadie: How do you sign up for that newsletter again?

Keep in touch with the girls!

Sign up for our newsletter at www.greenwomanmagazine.com

Bee in Cherry Blossoms by Leslie Macon

Uncle Joe's Onions

by James Ciletti

Right after mass and communion on St. Patrick's day, with
big snowflakes fluttering down on him, Uncle Joe's
foot and spade were turning over his garden.
With a sharp stick he furrowed long rows of black earth
then drilled hole after hole and
planted and covered white onion bulbs.

When the rains kept him in, he pulled back the curtain
and in his mind's eye I'm sure he saw the long white
fingers of onions growing deep into the dark earth.
By late April, he knelt on one knee and tugged weeds
from between new green onion stalks.

In early May, knowing the work of sun and rain,
knowing as only Uncle Joe could know, he dug
his shovel deep into the earth to turn out a dozen onions.

First, holding them up to the sun, then tapping off
the dirt, pulling off the first outer skin,
cutting off the hairy roots, and at the spigot,
washing the onions and his hands in cold water.

Up in the kitchen he shook salt over an onion,
bit, then chewed and closed his eyes. Smiling,
he remembered the snowflakes,
and received communion, again.

Gardening with the Moon
by Rebekah Shardy

"The Wandering Moon" by William Blake, illustration to John Milton's "L'Allegro" and "Il Penseroso" (1816-20)

"The Moon's a harsh mistress. She's hard to call your own." Jimmy Webb

More aptly, we have been the moon's mistress for the past 4.5 billion years, ever since earth's gravity pulled her as a meandering asteroid into our orbit (the spouse theory), or she was flung into being at the same time as our genesis from the Big Bang (the sister theory). I prefer the Romantic idea that a glancing blow from galactic collision spun a piece off the earth into space beside us (the daughter theory), so that when we look at the moon we actually peer into our own ancient past.

The Moon's beginnings are a mystery and so is the fundamental question: what would life be like on Earth without her? Would fertility falter, plants wither, seas turn to slime, and the soul suffer?

Scientists widely agree the moon affects tides, but the idea that it can shape human emotion or behavior is ridiculed as "the Transylvanian Effect." There may be good reason to disdain the possibility of lunar persuasion on human behavior. What chaos would result if defense attorneys claimed the moon phase as culprit in murder cases? Humans prefer to think they control nature, not the other way around, despite anecdotal evidence from police stations and emergency rooms to suggest otherwise.

At least two studies have examined the power of the moon over plants. I am the most recent woman in my family—from who knows how many before my grandmother?—to plant by the moon year after year with stunning results.

The Moon and Motherwit

My grandmother, born prior to 1900, was an over-achiever by any generation's standards. She birthed 13 children and cared for a blind father and consumptive sister-in-law until their deaths; traveled a circuit to sell dry goods to supplement her husband's income as a carpenter; played the violin and wrote plays; and was apprenticed as a midwife and healer—herbal and magic—in her country village.

She died before I was born in 1956 but my mother told me how she sifted garden soil with a screen until it was as "fine as cake flour." This was before the advent of pesticides and she had her own biological weapon: a pet toad who patrolled her rows to pluck rogue invaders with its dead-aim tongue.

"She also planted by the moon," my mother said, and I wondered what that meant. I envisioned a witchy-woman sowing at midnight. Not so. It wouldn't make sense to me until later when I studied the moon's phases, a kind of celestial dance that also serves as metaphor for a woman's life, and all the changes that cycle through our time on earth.

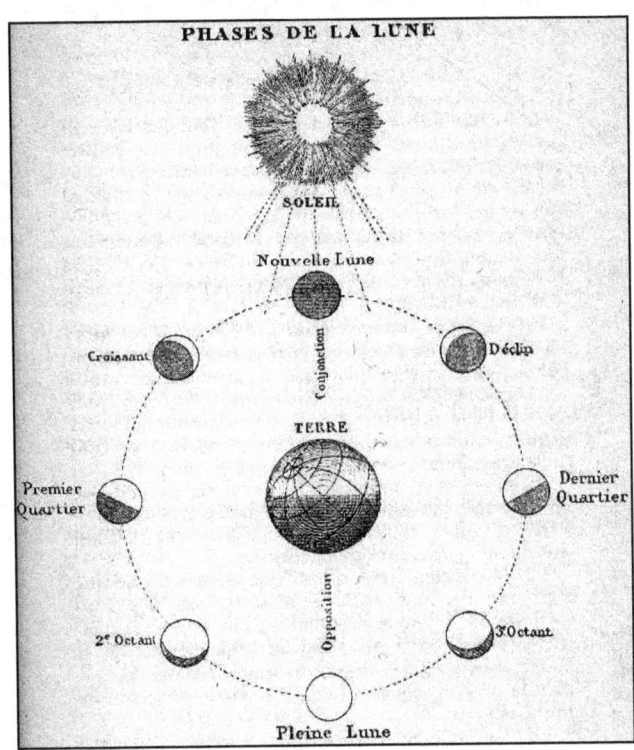

From *From the Earth to the Moon*, Henri de Montaut, 1868

The Faces (Phases) of the Moon

Our early ancestors were sky watchers as well as earth observers who made astute connections between the two. They noted life above and below is cyclical: spring is followed by summer, and summer by fall and winter. Young life is born, grows to maturity, and then withers in old age and dies. Change is constant, but you can predict it by observing the ordered circle of life's seasons.

The Moon demonstrates the lineage of transformation. When the moon is new (only a slim portion is lit by the sun), it appears as slender as a young girl—a coy curve in the sky. The New Moon was considered lucky. If you made a wish while holding a silver coin at first sight of the New Moon, your desire could come true. Eskimos believed they could catch more seals in the spring if they brought snow into their igloos when the moon was new. In parts of Africa, healing ceremonies began at the New Moon. I find it is a great time to set fresh goals and start new projects.

Just as girls become women and mothers, the New Moon grows larger (waxing) to half size (first quarter) and then is as full as a pregnant woman. In many cultures, the Full Moon was considered the time of manifestation for intentions established at the New Moon (a period of about two weeks). It was also a powerful time for using psychic abilities. And for the Greeks, the full moon was the luckiest, the 'blessed season' for marriage.

After the full moon's crowning fulfillment, it begins to shrink (waning) as a woman does toward old cronehood. Again it looks half (third quarter), then becomes so withered it appears to not exist at all (the Dark Moon). Early peoples saw the Dark Moon as a dangerous time when they were vulnerable to illness and evil; many spent the day in prayer, fasting, and other religious ceremonies for protection.

The Chinese Taoists point to the moon's phases as a lesson in natural balance: what is full must be made empty, and if you empty something it has the chance to become full. The balance of the universe depends on the cycle of change; we are wise to move with it, acquiring or letting go at the right times, accepting death and loss as much as life and gain. As long as the wheel of Life turns, excessive despair or pride is foolish. Wisdom serenely accepts the tides' inevitable ebb and flow.

So How Is It (Gardening with the Moon) Done?

My mother's instruction from her mother was simple:

1) If the fruit, produce or herb is above ground (cucumbers, tomatoes, rosemary, beans, etc,) sow the seed and harvest the results at the time when the moon is at least starting to wax after the First Quarter Moon and no later than the 2nd day of the Full Moon. Flowers are above the ground so this applies to them too. I planted my first garden during a full Super Moon in the month of May—the Flower Month in some Native American beliefs—and the results were phenomenal, especially my sunflowers. During a Super Moon, the moon is closer to the earth and 20% brighter.

Why do this? At the full moon, the sun and moon are on opposite sides of the earth, both pull with maximum light and magnetism. It is believed they not only raise tides at this time, but also pulling sap upward to the top of trees and plants. Medieval woodcutters avoided cutting trees at the Full Moon because they found the wood was too wet to burn well.

2) If the produce or herb is below the ground (radishes, beets, onions, burdock root, etc.) sow the seed and harvest the results no earlier than the Third Quarter Moon and no later than the Dark Moon. Transplanting (also affecting the roots), weeding and pruning are also effective if done during this time of decrease.

Why do this? Just as the Full Moon pulls sap upward in the tops of plants, sap settles down into the roots at the Dark Moon. It is believed this makes root vegetables and root herbs sowed and harvested at this time more potent and tasty. I don't like to cut trees, but if I have to do it, I prefer the Dark Moon in winter when the tree's energy is contained in the roots, as I believe trees are sentient and I want to reduce their suffering.

Goodnight, Moon

I am grateful to the moon for boosting my organic front yard gardens, so abundant that they attracted local press and fed neighbors, friends, bees, birds, and butterflies, entirely without the help of fertilizers. Organic gardening is tough, and we need all the tools we can find to do it well. Gardening with the moon won't replace the benefits of good soil, adequate water and hard work, but it will help you achieve your best results.

And it is a lovely way to wed the sky with the earth. For ages, humans have forged a personal relationship with their closest celestial body (220,000 to 250,000 miles from us depending on its ellipsis), through diverse human endeavors such as gardening, poetry, romance, and religion. The strangest moon ritual I've heard is that of rural Sicilian women going topless and chanting a special song to the full moon in the belief that it increased breast size! Perhaps there is a lunar recipe somewhere for erectile dysfunction, or so last year's zucchini would suggest.

The moon has especially touched religion with its radiance. Besides pagans who have worshipped the moon—as god or goddess depending on the culture—it holds a special place in Buddhist hearts. Gautama became the transcendent Buddha as he sat meditating beneath a tree under a Full Moon. In a lovely Zen story, a poor, wandering nun, banished from a village where she longed to sleep for the night, woke up under a cherry tree and the Full Moon. She was amazed by the beauty of the sky, and attained Enlightenment by realizing:

"Through their kindness in refusing me lodging
I found myself beneath the blossom of the night of this misty moon.
We become Buddhas the moment we accept all that life brings with gratitude."

My own spiritual connection with the moon was born when my infant son in my arms pointed to the sky and said, "Ball." I gave him the moon's name and whispered:

I see the Moon and the Moon sees me;
God bless the Moon, and God bless me.

You and your gardens too. ❀

Rockwell Kent, *Wilderness* (1920), *Woman*

The Moon Loves a Garden
A Relationship in Three Phases

by Rebekah Shardy

Dark Moon

Blink back those biting tears:
The lover's bed is all unmade, disheveled by divorce.
Where bees nibbled the basil's blooms—now brown withering of desire.
The beanpoles are aslant as words half said/misunderstood.
The sunflowers—once optimistic, extravagant as passion—
stiffen, skeletal. Aborted in its making, a squash blossom stops,
twists into blighted wan fruit; freak that's neither food nor flower.

New Moon

Dressed in white I bring with me the morning:
Thanking the places that pearled into purple bean flowers,
now frosted with memory; yet heart is warmed by the scarlet stems
of swiss chard harvested and holy to the nub.
Long squash arms, emerald and whole then, now tangled snakes seeking
return to deep earth; now is the time to be brave, I say, to them and me,
collecting the silent promise of seeds, good secrets, charred gold.

Full Moon

Please take me with you, they all said:
So I swirled olive oil in the shining pan to glisten and bless
the tang of chard and garlic; later the happy yellow squashes
commingled with sweet onion and bright-fleshed tomatoes.
Basil hangs in the window where satisfied Selene spies.
The lemon balm dries, waiting for the steaming cup of winter tea.
I will consume you all in perfect grace: Love is the honey long after the bee.

Cactus Carla by Laura Chilton

Cactus: Beyond the Phallus

by Elisabeth Kinsey

Sex
in the
Garden

If you don't die of thirst, there are blessings in the desert. You can be pulled into limitlessness, which we all yearn for, or you can do the beauty of minutiae, the scrimshaw of tiny and precise. The sky is your ocean, and the crystal silence will uplift you like great gospel music, or Neil Young.
—Anne Lamott

There are the obvious sexual euphemisms with cacti, since they're horny, they stick straight out and they protrude in general. But when I was twelve, we moved to Tucson, Arizona, from California, and seeing a cactus was a new phenomenon for me. Instead of the green pastures I used to roll down, the new terrain inserted danger into the landscape. I had to be surefooted, or I'd get hurt. My first exposure to nudity was Rueben's flaccid examples in *Fall of the Damned*. In Tucson, the Sonoran Desert Museum and even the Tanque Verde Swap Meet (how Arizonans say "flea market") displayed tables' worth of the penis cactus, *Echinopsis lageniformisi*, or Bolivian Torch Cactus, pointing from pots. The body was comprised of two cactus limbs. One limb jutted perpendicular and was dressed in doll jeans, googly eyes glued to its head. It often wore a tiny cowboy hat. The other limb burst forth out of the middle of the jeans, prickly, with nothing adorning it. At twelve, my mind exploded. Cacti were naughty, and they were all around me. What other cacti could represent that body part, and how could I delve into the mysteries of life through cactus?

My mother had said over and over while commanding me to avert my eyes, "Those are dirty." What that did was make me more curious. In came a spree for me of being "interested" in what boys had, and how it worked with girls, and in what could possibly be the meaning behind this jutting and prickly thing and why it would be called "dirty." My mother took me out of sex-ed classes and ironically, in the library, I read terrible one-liner romance novels, where the women always had "nuggets of desire" instead of nipples, and the man's junk was called a "bulging member." So how could cactus, that dry and spiky plant that survives on very little water, be associated with a vibrant boy part?

In seventh grade, our homeroom teacher required all of us to go on desert walks and to write down every cactus we could match with our cactus guide book. They were mysterious: the ocotillo sprouting from its center and towering green octopus tendrils to the sky; the cholla, furry and sprawling, ready to "jump" into anyone's pant leg, which is how it was named "jumping cactus"; and, finally, the saguaro, an obvious phallus dotting all of Tucson's open space. If one has a good camera and a good angle, any photo could capture its obvious masculine presence.

This was the first year my hens and chicks had multiple shoots of chicks and the first year they sent a pink masterpiece into the sky. When I was growing up, my father kept a succulent garden, and I wondered if it was the same mechanism in cacti that caused this birthing. It turns out the succulents are closely related, but my mind was fixated on that first encounter with the penis cactus. I found a site boasting the "10 Most Suggestive Cacti on Earth." In it they include plenty of bulging and prickly characters. What I didn't expect to find was the cacti's "offshoots" in many cases were blooms, actually more of a female quality, but still bursting forth with phallic radiance. (Like the

> "Prickly pear was my favorite cactus . . . not only because it somehow produced red, pendulous fruit that converted itself into jam, but because if push came to shove, I could survive on that plant alone, a mother's milk of the desert."

Cephalocereus gaumeri whose hanging orbs could be construed as feminine or masculine, according to the stance you take.) In another cactus blog, *Lophophra*, I found its author professing the German version of the penis cactus (montrose Trichocereus bridgesii) as "*Frauenglück*" or "good luck to women," which suggests their purpose is more to serve women then as an attachment to a male body. The San Pedro (*Trichocereus pachanoi*) boasts nocturnal blooms and psychoactive quality. The aphrodisiac feature unites the sexes, and has been used medicinally by indigenous North Americans for centuries.

Prickly pear was my favorite cactus in my formative years, not only because it somehow produced red, pendulous fruit that converted itself into jam, but because if push came to shove, I could survive on that plant alone, a mother's milk of the desert. I had no idea back then that its flat paddles extended into weed-like expanses and prevented early European settlers from farming the land. If they only knew the life support they provided, perhaps they could have farmed them. Katherine Zeratsky, RD, LD claims the "Prickly pear cactus, also called nopales, is promoted for treating diabetes, high cholesterol, obesity, and hangovers. It is also touted for its antiviral and anti-inflammatory properties." If the early settlers knew about the prickly pear's bounty, perhaps we would have a different past.

Looking back on my piece-meal sexual introduction starting with the penis cactus and trashy romance novels, I am glad I've moved beyond that first swap meet table of knick-knack cacti. I appreciate the cactus for feminine life support, amidst the obvious phallus. ❋

Sources:

Indoor Office Plants: http://www.cactus-art.biz/schede/TRICHOCEREUS/Trichocereus_bridgesii/Trichocereus_bridgesii_mostruosa_B/Trichocereus_inemis_mostruosus_inemis_B_penis_cactus.htm

Ten Most Suggestive Cactus on Earth: http://www.environmentalgraffiti.com/featured/10-most-suggestive-cacti-on-earth/11423

Cactus blog: http://lophophora.blogspot.com/2005/10/how-penis-cactus-got-its-name.html San Pedro Cactus: http://sivasakti.com/articles/couple/aphrodisiacs-art90.html

Prickly Pear: Is Arsenic an Aphrodisiac?: The Sociochemistry of an Element edited by William R. Cullen.

by Mae Fayne & Angus Skillet

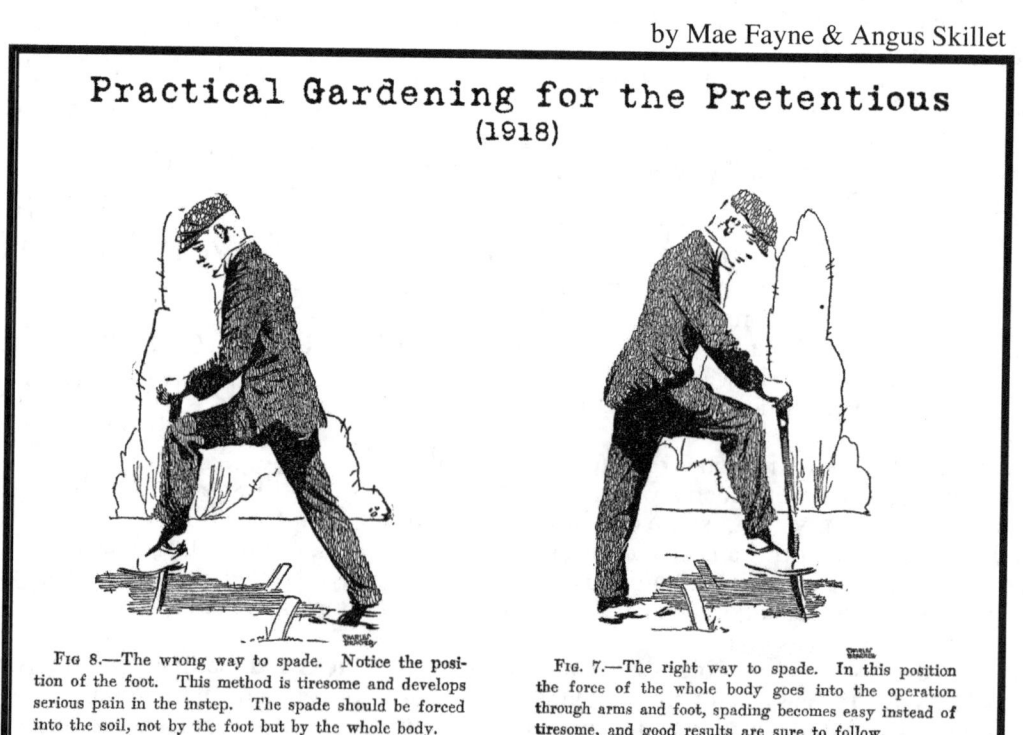

Practical Gardening for the Pretentious
(1918)

FIG 8.—The wrong way to spade. Notice the position of the foot. This method is tiresome and develops serious pain in the instep. The spade should be forced into the soil, not by the foot but by the whole body.

FIG. 7.—The right way to spade. In this position the force of the whole body goes into the operation through arms and foot, spading becomes easy instead of tiresome, and good results are sure to follow.

Ambrosius Bosschaert the Elder (1573-1621)
Bouquet of Flowers in a Glass Vase, 1621

Leafing Through
a review of books, etc.

Wonder: The Lives of Anna and Harlan Hubbard
Film. Written, Directed and Produced by Morgan Atkinson (Duckworks, Inc., 2012)

Anna and Harlan Hubbard were a couple who "dropped out" during the 1940s—a time when future baby boomer-back-to-the-landers were little more than a twinkle in their parents' eyes. Harlan, an artist, naturalist, writer and freedom-worshipper, and Anna, a scholar-librarian and Harlan's co-conspirator, accomplished with aplomb what few only dream of—living a life of true freedom and grace off the bounty of Nature. The twist is that they did so for over four decades and that, for five years, they did so while floating down a river on a shantyboat.

Harlan and Anna met in Cincinnati, Ohio, at the library where Anna worked. Both were in their early 40s and came from well-educated and accomplished families, hardly what you'd expect in future "river rats" (Harlan's term). They fell in love and spent the first two years of their marriage living in a riverbank shack, building a shantyboat and learning what they'd need to know for their adventure. They then took their creation down the Ohio River, and then the Mississippi, traveling from Cincinnati to New Orleans. They were true river people, drifting along with their dog, a johnboat, provisions, books, musical instruments, painting supplies, and a beehive, at a time when "river people" were on their

way to extinction. (This lifestyle was not uncommon in America's early days, folks going down the river with all their possessions and a crate or two of farm animals, looking for land on which to settle.)

Harlan, since childhood, perferred the wilds over civilization and yearned for the freedom that could only be found there. As the driving force behind the couple's adventure, he is also at the center stage in this film. You see his evolution as a painter, and as a person who crafts not only his own homes but his own life. He is the one with the vision and he tells most of the story. Wendell Berry, who wrote a book about Harlan Hubbard, narrates this film, which is written largely from quotes from Harlan's journals and Berry's book. Anna is shown as the woman who encourages Harlan and helps him realize his dreams.

After their years on the river, the Hubbards buy a piece of land in Payne Hollow, Kentucky. There they build an artistically-constructed home and grow their own produce and raise goats for meat, cheese, and milk. They also forage and fish, gleaning free sustenance from the river and surrounding lands. All their needs are met with apparently little income from the outside world (this is, unfortunately for the curious, something that is not explored in any depth). Their home does not have electricity or most modern "conveniences" although, like the boat, it is filled with what matters: art, books, and music (both Anna and Harlan play instruments and Anna has a Steinway piano).

I had several questions after viewing this film—for example, how they grew and canned their own food while on the river. It was said they had gardens when they set anchor in the warm seasons, yet there were no details. (I later found these questions answered in Harlan's book *Shantyboat*.) But the main thing I wondered about was Anna. For her, was this life fulfilling? There are a couple of passing mentions that life was not always easy, and Harlan himself wonders about the effect of their life on his wife's overall happiness, but it's only a mention.

In spite of these questions, I loved *Wonder*. This beautifully crafted, elegant film by Morgan Atkinson leaves you contemplating the deeper meaning of life, the definition of freedom, and what it would be like to attempt a real adventure—one that requires all your abilities as a human being. It is obvious that the Hubbards lived with grace and were one with the land. This film will make

some of us yearn for a taste of that experience. As far as contentment, I would think they solved that problem too, for the most part, as much as humans ever do.
—*Sandra Knauf*

Plastic Free: How I Kicked the Plastic Habit and How You Can Too
by Beth Terry
(Skyhorse Publishing, 2012)

I was introduced to Beth Terry's book by her website http://myplasticfreelife.com, formerly the blog, Fake Plastic Fish. Terry's 2007 epiphany about her plastic usage both surprised me and made me stop and think about how much plastic my family was using without giving much thought.

As someone who is not a fan of plastic, preferring natural materials, I make a conscious effort not to bring plastic into my home. But when you start thinking about the everyday plastics Americans are surrounded with and accept as part of life, the list of plastics becomes overwhelming. We dutifully (try to) take our reusable fabric bags to the supermarket and farmers' markets to avoid using plastic bags, recycle what plastics our area recyclers collect, drink coffee and water out of reusable containers and try to purchase items that are minimally packaged. But what about personal care products, CD cases, office supplies, cleaning products, synthetic clothing and foot ware, restaurant take out containers, stickers on supermarket fruits and vegetables and a myriad of other plastic items we think we can't live without? Or haven't tried to?

Written in the same light, conversational tone as her blog and website, Terry encourages readers to first take the "Show Your Plastic Challenge" as an important "awakening" step in addressing their plastic usage. She then offers small but meaningful examples on how to reduce, recycle, and "upcycle" existing plastics. Ten chapters take readers through a comprehensive overview of our dependance on plastics and give many real world examples of simple changes that aren't the usual ideas we are used to hearing. The book covers the basics of plastic: types, problems, environmental impact of recycling, less-plastic grocery shopping and household cleaning, and

keeping motivated on reducing your usage. Terry encourages readers so that they can make worthwhile personal changes without inducing eco-guilt. Inspiring Plastic-Free and Less-Plastic Hero profiles (ordinary individuals who have made kicking the plastic habit a way of life and promoted big changes in their communities) are interesting anecdotes that illustrate how powerful simple change can be.

The addition of personal stories, helpful sources (including websites and plastic-free products), photographs and tips on taking action in your home and your community make this a extensive resource book for every level, from kids who are concerned for their planet to community groups who want to make a real difference.

At the end of each chapter, Terry offers an Action Items Checklist, steps that can help you live a life less dependent on plastic. She challenges the reader to choose a step that might "feel a little more difficult."

Whether you choose to embrace a complete plastic-free life or just would like to know the options, *Plastic Free*, is both a practical and an inspiring guide.
—*Pat Kennelly*

The Roots of My Obsession
Edited by Thomas C. Cooper
(Timber Press, 2012)

What would you say if you had about a thousand words to explain why you do something that you are intensely passionate about—something to which you have devoted a significant portion of your life? Thomas C. Cooper, former editor of *Horticulture* magazine, gave thirty gardeners that opportunity by asking them specifically why they garden. He then published their responses in a book called, *The Roots of My Obsession: Thirty Great Gardeners Reveal Why They Garden*. The answers he got were varied, of course, but they all seemed to have the same underlying theme: an ineffable desire and drive to be connected to other living things—as if they were destined to garden.

Explaining this "destiny" was the challenge. Most

responders brought up stories from their childhoods, pivotal moments that put them on the path to becoming dedicated gardeners as adults. As a child, Rosalind Creasy was tasked with removing cutworms from her father's tomato plants. The response she received from her father each time she removed a cutworm made her feel as though she "had saved the family from starvation." In his formative years, Panayoti Kelaidis simultaneously assisted and annoyed his older sister's husband in the construction of a large rock garden. This experience eventually resulted in Kelaidis landing a job as the curator of an alpine garden at a prominent botanical garden.

A few responses to Cooper's question demonstrated that a love for plants doesn't necessarily have to be at the center of a love of gardening. Roger B. Swain's love of eating fruit is what motivates him. Douglas W. Tallamy is passionate about wildlife, and so his gardens are designed to be a habitat for critters.

Another major theme that is woven throughout this book is that gardeners are in it for life – probably because there is always more to do. Amy Stewart affirms that the word "'garden' is a verb, not a noun," and so she continues on "tinkering with the plant world" as humans have done for so many generations. Ken Druse gardens on an island on the East Coast, and so he faces, among numerous other things, the threat of regular floods, yet he "keep[s] coming back to the land" to put it all back together again every time disaster strikes.

If I were to be asked Cooper's question with my response limited to a few short pages, I would be stumped. How does one distill that kind of passion into a statement so succinct and definitive? These thirty gardeners gave it a great effort though, and their essays are bound to be both relatable and inspiring to anyone who has devoted their life to digging in the dirt.

—Dan Murphy

Beatrix Potter's Gardening Life: The Plants and Places That Inspired the Classic Children's Tales
by Marta McDowell
(Timber Press, 2013)

I didn't know Beatrix Potter's books as child, but later I read my girls tales of Peter Rabbit, the Flopsy bunnies, Jemima Puddleduck, Jeremy Fisher and the rest. We had a menagerie of animals (including a rabbit, or two, depending on the year) and a garden, so Potter's imagination hit home with us in a big way.

A little later I'd learn about this storyteller's life through the 2006 film *Miss Potter*, with Renée Zellweger and Ewan McGregor. It too charmed, and I was impressed with the story of a Victorian-era woman who, against the odds, became successful in her art and, more importantly, claimed power over her life.

Marta McDowell's newest book focuses on this notable life via a gardening path. Readers will delight in learning about the young Beatrix's development as an artist (by age 10 her drawings of plants were showing promise), the gardens she played in, and the holiday residences in Scotland where she first found inspiration in nature. Later they will see how she develops into an adult who, through the success of her art, is able to create a life of meaning, beauty, and self-sufficiency in England's Lake District.

I sat down with this book on a warm Sunday morning in November and spent a day immersed in Potter's world, taking breaks only to get some exercise outside—digging new vegetable and flower beds.

Much of the book enchants, but the eye-opener for me was learning about Potter's passion for mycology (the study of fungi) in her 20s and early 30s. At this point (before Peter Rabbit) she was a serious scholar and botanical artist and even presented a paper in 1897, "On the Germination of the Spores of the Agaricineae," to the Linnean Society. She might have made botany, or botanical illustration, her life's work if her foray into the field had not been thwarted by the male establishment (Kew botanist George Massee presented the paper for her because, as a female, Potter could not attend proceedings or read her own paper). Fortunately for children the world over, but perhaps sadly for Potter, her paper did not go further. This setback led her directly to children's literature. (According to author Linda Lear, who wrote *Beatrix Potter: A Life in Nature*, the Linnean Society issued an posthumous apology to Potter in 1997 for the sexism displayed in its handling of her research.)

After her success with *The Tale of Peter Rabbit*, Potter bought her first home, Hill Top Farm. It consisted of 34 acres. There she would raise animals, have an orchard, and do everything else one associates with country life. Eventually she acquired over 4,000 acres of land and more small farms in the area. At her death she bequeathed this property to the United Kingdom's National Trust for preservation—I saw it as the ultimate honor of her life's passion for nature.

McDowell's book is comprehensive. The first half of the book is a portrait of Potter's lifetime of growth as an artist, nature-lover, gardener, and woman. Part II describes her gardens through the seasons, and Part III details how to visit these gardens if you are fortunate enough to be able to visit her part of the U.K. As if that weren't quite enough, McDowell includes at the end of the book a listing of almost 20 pages of plants Potter mentions in correspondence and creates in her art.

I loved this book and would recommend it to Beatrix Potter fans, those who adore true cottage-style gardening, nature lovers, and those who relish a great story about a woman of immense talent, imagination, and enterprise.
—*Sandra Knauf*

Seeing Flowers: Discover the Hidden Life of Flowers
Written by Teri Dunn Chace; Photography by Robert Llewellyn
(Timber Press, 2013)

"We've all seen red roses, blue irises, and yellow daffoils. But when we really look closely at a flower, whole new worlds of beauty and intricacy emerge."
—Teri Dunn Chace

There are over 340 flower photographs in *Seeing Flowers*, and they are *stunning*. They were generated by Robert Llewellyn who, in his previous book *Seeing Trees*, had pioneered the method of using multiple images shot from different focus points. These images are then stitched together using software developed from work with microscopes. This technique gives us detailed images that show the anatomical parts of the flowers better than we can see them up close. We can also see the texture of these flowers, the thinness or thickness of the petals, the fuzziness of the leaves, and the subtleties in color variation. All parts of the flower are in focus, making these photographs more lifelike than traditional macro-photography.

The images themselves take up about one half of this three-hundred page book. The photographs are displayed on white backgrounds, and the book itself is good-sized

(about 8" x 9") with glossy paper. The beauty of these photographs, combined with accompanying quotes about specific flowers—by writers such as Goethe, Shakespeare, and some famous moderns—give this book a charming and romantic background that balances the informational text by Teri Dunn Chace.

The book is organized into sections of the 28 most common and studied flower families, such as *Amaryllidaceae*, *Hydrangeaceae*, and *Rosaceae*. The book includes a diverse body of information. It describes the most common flowers in each family and gives the reader examples of how one can see that common flowers are related in a family. Chace includes historical and legendary information relating to these plants: how people explained the appearance of certain flowers, how they were named, etc. One legend I found interesting was the explanation for the small purple flower commonly found in the center of Queen Anne's lace—according to lore, Queen Anne pricked her finger during the intricate process of making lace, and the tiny flower represents a drop of royal blood (the colored flower actually serves to attract insects). The book also includes medicinal and psychiatric uses for some of these plants, harmful effects of certain flowers, geographic locations, information for hybridizing varieties, and growing conditions.

If you don't know much about botany, I suggest brushing up on key concepts—volatile oils, hybridization, pollination, and fertilization—before reading *Seeing Flowers* in order to get the most out of the text.

With the holidays coming up, I would recommend this book as a gift for anyone interested in botany, photography, gardening, or simply the enchanting beauty of flowers.
—*Zora Knauf*

Top Dressing

Nurture, Nurture, Nurture by Kathryn Hall

Near as I can tell life on planet Earth is mostly about taking care. Taking care of our families. Taking care of our friends. Taking care of the work that is our responsibility. Taking care of our homes, taking care of our possessions, our animals, our gardens, our plants, our cars, our water, our air, our land. Our churches, our communities, our cities our roads, our poor, our sick, our wounded, our frail and elderly. Taking care of ourselves. Taking care of ourselves physically. Taking care of ourselves mentally. Taking care of ourselves spiritually.

Now, how we go about that is endless as its possibilities. As varied as the fish in the sea, the birds in the sky, the plants in the forest. And notice they are all taking care as well.

If I ask myself what is the central principle behind this endless and perpetual taking care, I'd have to say life itself. Life reaching towards life. Life ensuring life continues. That, essentially, is the drive behind it all, is it not? Each and every living thing on planet Earth is hardwired for doing well, for keeping the whole thing going, for perpetuating life. The lengths various species go to ensure their sticking around boggles the mind.

As we are caught up in our own individual dramas and the illusions (and grandeurs) of our sense of separation, it is easy (and convenient) to forget what the essential driving force behind all this is. Truly there are beings walking planet Earth thinking it was about them. "What? It's not about me?" Well, it is. You and over six billion other people and a several billion other species. It is humbling to contemplate, when we take the time.

And the distorted ways in which some of us choose to take care of ourselves and others are absolute abominations, there is no doubt. But often underneath the aberration one could find this slender thread of life's longing at the core, hard as that might seem.

What would our lives look like if we consciously brought the value of taking care, of nurturing to the fore? How would aligning ourselves with that single focus impact our lives and the lives of others? If we acknowledged fully our intrinsic programming to care and nurture for all that came within our view, our path, our neighborhood, our own small radar, what impact would that accumulative shift have on our larger reality?

Jesus said to love one another. Was that not the same? ❋